THE BANGALORE CONSPIRACY

NISHEET KUMAR

Srishti
Publishers & Distributors

Srishti Publishers & Distributors
A unit of AJR Publishing LLP
212A, Peacock Lane
Shahpur Jat, New Delhi – 110 049

editorial@srishtipublishers.com

First published by Srishti Publishers & Distributors in 2025

10 9 8 7 6 5 4 3 2 1

"In a world built on silence,
even one true voice
can change everything."

To

Jai Shri Guru Maharaj Ji!

"Srimad J.G.R. Swami Shri Purushottamacharya Ji Maharaj"

my light & my compass

My family—my soul, the roots of my being.

To my mother and father.

To Babita, Aarjav & Arushi,

and my extended family—the circle that holds me.

Author's Note

Stories are often born not from sudden brilliance, but from long conversations, observations, and silent battles fought within us.

The Bangalore Conspiracy began as a simple idea, a desire to weave together the worlds I know intimately: policing, corporate affairs, and the rapidly evolving field of artificial intelligence. As a senior police officer, I have witnessed both the fragility and the resilience of security systems. My professional experience in public governance, alongside my close association with the corporate world, has shown me how ambition, ethics, and rivalry can dangerously flirt with betrayal.

This novel was seeded in deep discussions with my son Aarjav, who has a background in computer science, AI, and management. His insights into technology, paired with my experiences from the field, created fertile ground for thoughtful fiction. We envisioned a story where modern threats extend beyond bullets and boardrooms to encompass data, ambition, and the invisible wars waged in coded silence.

This is not merely a tale of conspiracy; it is a reflection on trust, courage, and resilience, values that matter just as much on the streets of Bangalore as they do in the glass towers of global corporations.

I owe gratitude to my family, whose belief in this journey never wavered; to my colleagues in policing and corporate circles who, knowingly or unknowingly, inspired this narrative; and to you, the reader, for choosing to step into this world with me.

As you turn these pages, I invite you not only to chase the thrill of the story but also to reflect: In a world fuelled by ambition and fear, who truly holds the power?

And who dares to challenge it?

Dr Nisheet Kumar

Chapter 1

BANGALORE RISING

The Bangalore skyline gleamed behind the glass walls of the tech arena, bathed in the warm hues of a setting sun. Inside, anticipation simmered like static before a lightning strike. The air buzzed not just with technology but with ambition, strategy, and rivalry.

TechNova's flagship event was more than a product launch; it was a showdown, a spectacle where companies flaunted their power and vision, and where reputations could be elevated or dismantled in real-time.

A staff member whispered into his microphone, "Ten seconds to walk-in."

Behind the curtain, Aryan Mehra adjusted the cuffs of his navy suit. He wasn't nervous; his mind was sharp and focused.

Rajeev Menon stood beside him, scrolling through a final diagnostic on his tablet. "You know Vihan Sethi is in the front row, don't you?" he said casually.

"NeuroVista's golden boy. He's probably praying you trip over a cable."Aryan smirked. "Let him pray. He's launching a glorified health app with a fancy interface. Mediscan is going to rewrite diagnostics."

"Sure, but be prepared, he might come at you during the Q&A. You know how he likes drama."

Aryan shrugged. "Let him do so. The truth doesn't need defence; it just needs clarity."

He looked out at the crowd gathering beyond the curtain. Executives from competing firms, government health officials, venture capitalists, AI ethics panels, and international media—all had a stake in what TechNova would unveil today.

And TechNova itself? Once a mid-tier software outfit, Aryan had transformed it into a global name in AI-driven healthcare solutions within five years. From predictive analytics in urban trauma centres to low-cost mobile diagnostic kits in tribal belts, TechNova wasn't just competing, it was disrupting.

Rajeev leaned closer. "Your microphone's hot in ten seconds. Do you want to start with the AI story or the emotional pitch?"

Aryan exhaled slowly. "Start with the why. Then hit them with the how."

Rajeev grinned. "That's the Aryan I know."

A soft cue light blinked above, and the stage manager gave the nod.

Aryan stepped forward, the light catching his face as he walked into view.

And just like that, Bangalore held its breath.

Aryan Mehra strode onto the stage, and the applause rolled through the auditorium like thunder on a monsoon night. His polished black Oxfords tapped against the floor with confidence, yet each step masked the undercurrent of adrenaline surging beneath his calm exterior.

He was the man of the moment, the face of India's tech renaissance. As the CEO of TechNova, Aryan exuded authority and charm in equal measure. His tailored navy suit hugged his athletic frame, and under the glow of the spotlight, he looked more like a movie star than a tech visionary.

He paused at centrestage, scanning the packed hall at the Bangalore Tech Summit. From venture capitalists to students, policy makers to sceptics, everyone had their eyes locked on him. With a charismatic smile, he raised a hand to acknowledge the standing ovation.

"Good evening," he began, his baritone voice cutting through the noise like a conductor's baton commanding an orchestra. "Thank you for that generous welcome. I assume the free coffee at the stalls wasn't the only reason this hall is overflowing?"

Laughter rippled across the crowd, and Aryan let it settle.

He began pacing slowly, his eyes gleaming with intent. "We live in a world obsessed with speed," he began. "But the future doesn't just need to be fast, it needs to be intelligent."

He paused and clicked the remote in his hand. A dynamic visual appeared on the screen behind him, a circular schematic titled "Mediscan".

"Mediscan is not just a breakthrough; it's a transformation," he declared. "Imagine a system that doesn't just react to illness but predicts it. That learns with every heartbeat. That understands the language of disease before symptoms even surface."

He spoke in confident bursts; terms like 'deep learning', 'predictive diagnostics', and 'pattern-based inference' flowed effortlessly from him. However, underneath, Aryan knew he was walking a tightrope. The audience was with him now, but all it would take was one moment of doubt, one slip, to lose them.

"We've tested Mediscan in five rural clinics across three states. What we found was extraordinary. Yearly detection rates improved by 43 per cent. That's not just data; that's life. That's a mother seeing her child grow up. That's a father going back to work. That's hope."

Another round of applause broke out. Aryan let it wash over him.

But for a flickering moment, his eyes darkened, just a flash. He remembered his father's silent suffering, the too-late diagnosis, the helpless rage. That was why he had built this. That was what powered his conviction.

He raised his head again, his voice unwavering. "Mediscan is about giving people time to live, time to fight, time to choose. And today, we offer that time to the world."

The lights behind him dimmed, leaving only Aryan in the spotlight. And as the crowd erupted once again, his gaze lingered not on the front row, but on the shadows beyond, on the possibility that not everyone applauding was genuinely cheering.

***

The screen behind Aryan transformed again, this time displaying a split-screen simulation, one side showing traditional diagnosis timelines and the other highlighting the real-time detection capabilities of Mediscan.

"This is the future of diagnostics," Aryan said, his voice steady and compelling. "We're not just enhancing healthcare; we're redefining access." He emphasized how Mediscan was designed to operate in low-bandwidth environments and required minimal technical training. "Whether it's a primary care unit in Hyderabad or a mobile clinic in Jharkhand, Mediscan works."

He shifted tone, allowing vulnerability to seep into his polished delivery. "This isn't just about smart machines. It's about equity. It's about levelling the playing field because where you're born should never determine whether you live."

He shared a case study about an 8-year-old girl in Bihar whose tumour was detected in time, thanks to Mediscan's pilot run. Her photo appeared on the screen, showing her healthy and smiling.

The audience was silent, captivated. Aryan allowed the image to linger, giving them time to absorb the gravity of what they were seeing. Then, with quiet determination, he added, "She gets to live. That's what this is all about."

The spotlight shifted as Aryan clicked to the next slide, a layered diagram of Mediscan's architecture.

"Let's briefly discuss how Mediscan actually works," he said, the energy in his voice shifting from visionary to scientific. The audience leaned in.

"Mediscan is built on a three-tiered AI architecture. The first layer is pattern recognition, trained on over twenty million anonymized case files across eight geographies. This isn't just symptom matching; it's micro-anomaly detection, even in pre-symptomatic phases."

He paused, then zoomed in on a heatmap showing tissue-level deviations. "The second tier is probabilistic diagnosis. It uses Bayesian inference and deep clustering to offer a 'most likely' condition, but it doesn't stop there."

Aryan turned to face the crowd. "We built a third-tier human override model. Mediscan always flags high-sensitivity cases to certified physicians before any decision tree activates. This is so because AI must assist, not replace."

A hand shot up. Dr Aarti Kapoor, a public health researcher Aryan recognized. "Does it adapt to regional variations—dietary, genetic, and environmental?" she asked.

"Absolutely," Aryan responded. "We built local learning loops. The system doesn't just scale; it localizes. In Rajasthan, it accounts for fluoride exposure. In Kerala, it adjusts for coastal humidity and vector-based illnesses."

A murmur of appreciation rippled through the auditorium.

"Think of it as a diagnostic lens that sharpens over time," Aryan continued. "In a pilot run in Chhattisgarh, we identified twelve cases of early-stage pancreatic cancer that traditional screenings missed. All twelve patients are in recovery today."

The crowd remained quiet, then someone clapped, followed by another. The sound grew. Aryan let the applause swell, but then lifted a hand to regain the crowd's attention. "One more thing," he said. "Mediscan's real strength lies in time. Traditional diagnosis takes hours, sometimes days. With our system, real-time scans can be processed in under 180 seconds. Because early intervention doesn't wait."

Rajeev watched from the wings, whispering to a crew member, "He's not just pitching, he's rewriting the playbook."

In the audience, a rival CTO leaned toward his colleague. "He's getting too far ahead. We can't let this run unchecked."

Offstage, Rajeev Menon was juggling cables and code. Tall, wiry, with an infectious grin, and a lanyard covered in doodles, he was the tech whisperer of the operation. "He's brilliant," he muttered to himself, watching Aryan engage the crowd. But then his screen blinked; one of the demo nodes was lagging. "Seriously? Now?" he hissed.

He bent over his laptop, fingers a blur. Nearby crew members looked tense, but Rajeev's signature calm humour kicked in. "Relax. It's just the universe testing my patience. Again."

Back on stage, Aryan pressed on, unaware of the glitch. Rajeev launched into a soft diagnostic protocol while pretending to sip from an empty coffee cup. “Code and caffeine, my oldest love story,” he quipped to no one in particular.

Just as the display threatened to stall, Rajeev gave a subtle nod, a silent all-clear only Aryan would catch when their eyes briefly met, years of trust compressed into a glance. Aryan, still mid-pitch, gave the slightest smirk. He adjusted his microphone and continued. Together, they had pulled off this high-wire act dozens of times, but today’s stakes felt different. Neither of them could afford to miss a step.

***

Aryan stepped forward again, inviting questions from the audience with an open gesture. “Let’s hear your thoughts,” he said. “Innovation is a dialogue, not a monologue.”

A hand shot up, from a young researcher in the third row. “How do you ensure Mediscan doesn’t overdiagnose or trigger false alarms?”

Aryan smiled, nodding at the thoughtful question. “That’s a valid concern. Mediscan uses cross-referenced datasets and a second-layer confirmation loop. Think of it as an AI second opinion before raising any flags. We’ve built in guardrails.”

Another voice chimed in. “Is it affordable for rural deployment?”

Aryan’s expression shifted subtly, moving from confident to earnest. “We’ve partnered with government health schemes and NGOs to bring costs down. The goal is scalability without compromising quality. Healthcare access should never be a privilege.”

Laughter broke out when someone called out, “Will it work on my mother-in-law’s hypochondria?”

Aryan chuckled. “Only if she agrees to the terms and conditions.”

The room warmed again. He had the ability to toggle between technical gravitas and light-hearted charm with surgical precision. This was his arena.

The stage lights shifted to a cooler hue as Aryan raised the remote again. “Let’s stop imagining and see it in action.”

The screen behind him filled with a live demo feed. An anonymized patient scan loaded in real-time was displayed, with

Mediscan's interface displaying layered data—vitals, risk markers, and projected diagnostics.

Aryan spoke calmly, guiding the audience through it. "Here's where the anomaly surfaced before traditional symptoms even appeared. Our AI isolates micro-patterns the human eye might miss. This isn't a replacement; it's an augmentation."

Gasps echoed through the auditorium as Mediscan flagged an invisible risk marker. A wave of fascination moved through the room.

Aryan let the moment breathe.

"This is why we built it," he said softly. "For the edge cases. For the almost-missed diagnoses. For the people who didn't get their tomorrow."

He stepped back from the screen, letting the technology speak for itself.

The crowd erupted into applause.

Aryan smiled, but something within him stirred, pride, yes, but also a flicker of unease. What if the very power he'd created ended up in the wrong hands? What if trust in the system became blind?

He buried the thought, straightened his jacket, and raised the microphone again. "We call this hope. We call this 'Mediscan'."

The applause gradually faded, but a soft hum of energy remained, like static in the air. Aryan walked slowly toward the centrestage again, his tone shifting from inspirational to intimate.

"This isn't just innovation for its own sake," he began, his voice lower now, more personal. "This is about responsibility. It's about how we, the creators of technology, can choose to bend its arc toward good."

The screen now displayed a collage of snapshots from Mediscan's outreach programmes: a tent clinic in a dusty village, a smiling community health worker scanning a child, a mobile diagnostics van parked beside a paddy field.

"These aren't publicity shots," Aryan said. "They're proof. We've already deployed Mediscan in underserved areas across six states. Real places. Real people. Real lives changed."

He paused on one image, a gaunt man holding a printed scan report, his eyes wet with relief.

"He thought it was indigestion, but it wasn't. It was Stage II cancer. And he got treatment because our AI caught it."

The auditorium was silent. Aryan's voice dropped into a near-whisper. "We talk about disruption in tech. But this... this is disruption with dignity."

As he stepped back from the screen, the house lights came up slightly. Aryan removed the microphone from the stand and walked freely now.

The standing ovation that followed was slower, more emotional. People weren't just applauding the tech; they were applauding the intent.

Aryan gave a respectful nod, but his eyes drifted to the back of the auditorium as if seeking something. Or someone.

From the wings, Rajeev offered a silent thumbs-up and an exaggerated chef's kiss, mouthing, "Nailed it!"

Aryan grinned and walked offstage, the cheers still rising behind him.

Backstage, the noise dulled into a muffled roar. Rajeev met him halfway.

"I told you they'd lose their minds," he said.

"And here I thought I'd lose mine," Aryan replied with a half-laugh.

Rajeev clapped him on the shoulder. "That wasn't just a pitch, Aryan. That was a promise."

Aryan smiled, but the smile didn't fully reach his eyes. Something in him had shifted. The pride was still there, but now it was shadowed by the weight of expectation.

He pulled out his phone as they walked backstage together. A new message notification blinked on the screen.

He opened it, expecting a media inquiry. Instead, he read:

"Your empire is built on quicksand. Enjoy it while it lasts."

Aryan stopped walking. His stomach sank, not because of what the message said, but because of how specific it felt.

***

Rajeev leaned over to peek at Aryan's screen. "Spam?"

Aryan quickly locked the phone. "No. Just... unexpected feedback."

Rajeev raised an eyebrow. "Is it one of those anonymous 'you-changed-my-life' texts or the creepy 'I'm watching you' variety?"

Aryan forced a chuckle. "Somewhere in between."

They reached the press lounge, where a modest media crowd had already gathered. Lights flashed as Aryan entered, and a dozen recorders thrust forward like spears.

He stepped into the role with practised ease, masking the swirl of unease behind his signature poise.

"Mr Mehra, how do you address concerns that AI in diagnostics might replace doctors in underserved regions?" a journalist asked.

Aryan nodded thoughtfully. "Mediscan is not a replacement. It's a bridge between scarcity and access, between fear and clarity."

Another journalist chimed in, "What about data privacy? Some groups claim Mediscan's data lakes might be vulnerable."

Aryan's eyes flickered momentarily. "We've built the system on end-to-end encryption, with decentralization at its core," he replied. "No patient identity is ever stored. We're in the business of saving lives, not collecting profiles."

He continued, "In addition, multi-layered security audits are conducted quarterly by independent cybersecurity experts. We don't just rely on encryption; we challenge it relentlessly."

The words sounded solid, but the earlier message echoed louder now. Someone out there didn't believe in Mediscan's promise or didn't want the world to believe.

The conference lobby buzzed with energy as Aryan stepped away from the press area, with Rajeev walking right behind him.

"That was a good answer to the data privacy question," Rajeev said. "I thought it might be tricky."

Aryan smiled slightly. "If we can't answer hard questions, we shouldn't be building solutions."

A voice called out from behind, "Still giving deep quotes, Aryan?"

They turned around. By the refreshment table stood Vihan Sethi, well-dressed, confident, and grinning like he knew something others didn't. He was the CEO of NeuroVista. Aryan's old college friend was now his biggest rival.

"Vihan," Aryan said, shaking his hand. "Still testing jokes on your systems?"

Vihan returned the handshake quickly. "Only when I'm not running systems that are ten times faster than yours. That was a great show, though. You really played the hero card today."

Rajeev stepped forward with his arms folded. "It's nice of you to drop feedback from the cheap seats."

Vihan laughed. "I was in the front row, Rajeev. I couldn't miss the moment Aryan turned a stethoscope into a smart assistant."

Aryan didn't flinch. "Mediscan isn't replacing doctors; it's helping them. But you already know that. You just don't want your backers to know it."

The smile on Vihan's face tightened. He stepped a little closer. "Be careful, Aryan. Growing fast is risky. And not everyone watching is clapping; some are waiting."

Aryan stayed calm. "We're building with care. If someone's watching, let them. The ones copying usually clap the loudest."

Vihan's smirk faded briefly.

Rajeev added with a grin, "Enjoy your coffee, Vihan. We've got more people to impress."

As they walked off, Aryan remained silent. His face was calm, but his jaw had tightened.

Rajeev nudged him. "He's feeling the pressure. That backend comment was him trying to shake you."

Aryan nodded. "We're ahead, and he knows it. He's not just competing now; he's planning something."

He glanced at his phone, but there were still no new messages. But that old one echoed louder now. Quicksand. And now, a rival is watching every step. This wasn't just competition; it was the beginning of a deeper game, one that would pull Aryan into the tangled world of corporate agendas, secrets, and shadows.

And in the heart of Bangalore, the battle had only just begun.

***

After twenty minutes of polished responses, Aryan stepped aside, signalling the end of the media round.

He moved through the corridor connecting the lounge to the executive wing, more slowly now, less electrified by success.

In the hallway's polished glass, he caught his own reflection. For the first time that day, he saw the strain behind the charm, the exhaustion tucked neatly behind his collar.

A familiar voice called out. "Aryan!"

He turned to see Leena Varma, editor-in-chief of a major tech journal.

"That was a brilliant presentation," she complimented him. "Off the record, are you worried about rival companies trying to discredit you?"

He hesitated, just long enough for her to notice. "Only if I'm doing something worth discrediting."

She smiled. "Well, you certainly are."

They exchanged pleasantries, and then she disappeared into the crowd. Aryan stood still for a moment.

The message still burned at the back of his mind. It felt like not just a threat but a promise.

He opened his phone again. No follow-up. No sender details. Just that one line: "Your empire is built on quicksand."Aryan exhaled sharply.

For the first time that day, the applause felt far away.

Aryan returned to the executive green room, a modern lounge tucked away behind the main stage. The buzz of the conference hall dimmed to a low murmur behind soundproof doors.

He sank into a high-backed chair, but the weight of the message pressed harder now that the adrenaline had worn off.

Rajeev appeared with two bottles of water, tossing one to Aryan. "You were on fire out there," he said. "The Mediscan demo? Clean. Tight. Moving."

Aryan gave a tight smile. "Thanks. I'm just glad the servers didn't crash mid-scan."

Rajeev flopped onto the couch across from him. "So, what was that message?"

Aryan hesitated, then showed him the screen.

Rajeev's smile faded as he read it twice. "'Quicksand'? It sounds like someone's rattled. Anonymous, I assume?"

Aryan nodded. "No name. No number. Just a dead-end sender ID."

Rajeev leaned forward, his expression more serious now. "It could be a crank or someone testing the waters, checking your reaction. Either way, I don't like it."

"I'll have Kabir run a trace through our internal communications team," said Aryan. "Quietly."

"Do you want me to alert PR?"

"No. Not yet. If it's nothing, I don't want to give it oxygen. If it's something, we'll deal with it internally first."

The door opened again, and a junior assistant stepped in, handing Aryan a folder filled with press invites, follow-up media interactions, and congratulatory notes from corporate partners.

Aryan flipped through it mechanically, not really reading.

The warning replayed in his mind, more like an omen now than a threat: Your empire is built on quicksand.

He stared out the glass wall behind the lounge. From that vantage point, the view overlooked the heart of Bangalore's tech district, gleaming towers, solar panels, and traffic crawling below.

It looked like progress. It looked like permanence. But suddenly, it felt fragile.

His phone buzzed again. This time, it was a routine update from the company's internal dashboard.

Aryan sighed and stood up. "Let's wrap up the press follow-ups by evening. I need to clear my head."

Rajeev gave a mock salute. "Roger that, General."

As Aryan stepped out of the room, he paused for a second and glanced back. The chair he'd been sitting in was still spinning slightly for some reason, which unsettled him more than the message. It felt as though something had shifted and wouldn't quite settle again.

***

Aryan walked down the hallway with slower steps, the energy from the event dimming behind him. The digital walls replayed highlights of his keynote, soundless flashes of applause, and insight.

But his thoughts were elsewhere now: the message, the rival's warning, the growing feeling that something unseen had been set in motion.

He entered the executive lounge, a quieter space behind tinted glass. It smelled of polished wood and strong coffee. Alone, Aryan sat, scrolling again to the single message:

"Your empire is built on quicksand."

The words had transformed. They read like a warning. Or a countdown.

A gentle knock interrupted his thoughts. Rajeev entered without waiting. "I figured you'd be in here, trying to outthink a text."

Aryan didn't look up. "Wouldn't you?"

Rajeev sat opposite him, placing two cups of coffee on the table. "I'd call the number and offer them a demo."

Aryan smirked, but his face remained serious. "Do you think it's Vihan?"

Rajeev shrugged. "It's too dramatic for him. He likes credit. This feels… faceless."

Aryan leaned back, eyes on the ceiling. "It's just the beginning, Rajeev. We've hit the radar. Someone out there wants the storm to come faster."

Rajeev leaned forward. "Then let them come. But not before we tighten everything: tech, operations, and communications. No loose threads."

Aryan rose and walked to the floor-to-ceiling window. Bangalore stretched before him, endless buildings, blinking lights, ideas in motion. It looked solid. Secure. But he had built long enough to know how fragile foundations can be.

Behind him, Rajeev tapped away on his tablet, pulling up security and communications updates.

Aryan straightened his jacket. "Prepare a closed-door review with the leadership team for tomorrow morning."

"I'm on it," Rajeev replied.

Aryan took one last look outside. Bangalore had crowned him once. Now it might bury him. And Aryan Mehra intended to fight for every inch.

***

Chapter 2

THE SHIFTING GROUND

It had barely been twelve hours since Aryan had received a standing ovation at the Bangalore Tech Summit, but the applause had vanished like vapour. In its place was a digital wildfire.

He sat frozen in his cabin at TechNova's glass-walled headquarters in Whitefield, Bangalore. The headlines scrolled endlessly across his screen:

"BREAKING: Anonymous Whistleblower Alleges Data Manipulation in TechNova's Mediscan Project."

Rajeev burst in, face pale. "Aryan, it's everywhere: NDTV, CNBC, even Reddit. Someone dropped a full PDF of internal reports, flagged emails, and logs."

Aryan slowly turned to him. "Is the PDF real?"

Rajeev hesitated. "Some of the metadata matches," he replied. "But it's cherry-picked and twisted. It's not the full picture."

Aryan nodded once, then asked quietly, "Who sent it?"

"There was no name, just an anonymous email ID. But the tone is surgical. Like someone's been planning this for months."

Sanjay Kulkarni, TechNova's legal head, appeared in the doorway. "We need a statement. Now."

Aryan looked up. "A press note won't fix this."

"We can't stay silent either," Sanjay said. "Investors are calling. The Health Ministry is already asking questions."

Rajeev added, "The worst part is that some of our old internal QA reviews are in that dump, stuff we flagged and fixed. But out of context, they look damning."

Aryan leaned back, rubbing his eyes. "It's meant to create doubt. Not proof, just enough smoke."

Sanjay placed a draft statement on Aryan's desk. "At least, get ahead of the story. Reassure the public. We deny wrongdoing, highlight our ethics protocols, and maybe even reference the successes of the pilot programme."

Aryan scanned it briefly and shook his head. "It's too defensive. It reads like we're scared."

"So what do we say?" Rajeev asked.

Aryan looked at them both. "We speak from strength. We built Mediscan to save lives. That hasn't changed. Let's not act like we're hiding. We'll put our data model on the table and let it speak."

Rajeev nodded slowly. "Okay. That might work. But we'll need to prepare for fallout. This isn't just a PR crisis, Aryan. This feels like war."

Aryan's voice was calm but sharp. "Then let's prepare like it is."

***

The media frenzy outside TechNova headquarters had turned into a full-blown circus.

Reporters clustered around the gate, microphones raised like weapons. Security guards struggled to hold the line. News vans blocked the sidewalk, their satellite dishes pointed skyward.

Inside the building, a different storm brewed.

Aryan stood in the war room with his core team—Rajeev, Sanjay, and Anjali, the head of public relations.

Anjali was flipping through a printed Twitter feed. "#MediScam is trending," she said. "Thirty thousand mentions in two hours."

Rajeev muttered, "That's fast. Too fast. It feels coordinated."

Anjali looked up. "Do you think this was planted?"

Aryan nodded. "Whoever did this knew exactly where to hit. QA reports, metadata, internal review emails...this wasn't just a data leak. They framed a narrative."

Sanjay leaned against the table. "We need a press conference, not just a note. You, Aryan. Live. Transparent."

Aryan took a deep breath. "Fine. But no pre-scripted nonsense. I'll take questions. We'll project strength, not spin."

The press room was already packed by the time Aryan walked in.

There was a frenzy of flashes, and dozens of journalists pointed their cameras at him, notebooks ready to capture every word.

Aryan stood at the podium, flanked by Sanjay and Anjali.

"I know many of you have questions," he began. "And I won't read from a statement today. TechNova has nothing to hide."

Murmurs rippled through the crowd.

"Let me say this clearly," Aryan continued. "Mediscan has saved lives. Our pilot studies were peer-reviewed, our algorithms audited. And if anyone wants to see how the system works, we'll show you."

A reporter from NewsWire raised her hand. "What about the QA failures leaked today?"

"They were known, documented, and fixed months ago," Aryan said. "What's been leaked is only half the story, spun to look like fraud."

Another reporter shouted, "Are you saying this is a conspiracy?"

Aryan met her eyes. "I'm saying someone wants to stop Mediscan. And they're not afraid to play dirty."

The room fell into tense silence.

Aryan leaned into the microphone. "We won't be silenced by shadows. TechNova is here to stay."

He stepped back. The flashes resumed and so did the questions. Aryan had opened the floodgates, but he hadn't backed down.

Not yet.

***

Back in his office, Aryan removed the microphone from his collar and dropped it on the table.

Rajeev followed him in, shutting the door behind them. "You handled that like a pro," he said, though his voice was tight. "But we both know that was just Round One."

Aryan's shoulders sagged slightly. His hands, steady during the press conference, now trembled slightly, a silent admission of the toll the day had already taken on him. He leaned against the edge of the polished desk, fingers gripping its surface. "I've given them honesty. The rest is out of my control."

"But the market doesn't care about honesty," Rajeev said gloomily. "It cares about sentiment. And sentiment just tanked."

Aryan turned to the wall screen. A red graph was diving, TechNova's stock, in freefall.

"How much has it fallen?" he asked quietly.

Rajeev checked his phone. "Twelve per cent since this morning. Our board's in panic mode. VC calls haven't stopped."

Aryan exhaled heavily. "What about internal morale?"

Rajeev hesitated. "It's mixed. Some of the younger staff are scared. HR says two engineers resigned before noon. And there's a rumour going around that you're stepping down."

Aryan's eyes narrowed. "What?"

Rajeev nodded grimly. "It came from a spoofed internal mailer. IT's tracing it now."

Aryan straightened. "No one's stepping down. We fight this. I won't be another casualty in someone else's smear campaign."

Rajeev came closer and said in a low voice, "Then we need to fight smarter. Legal, PR, internal communications, all of it. There should be no gaps."

Aryan met his eyes. "We'll hold the line. Let them throw shadows, we'll stay in the light."

***

Aryan stared blankly at the screen, his vision blurring slightly as notifications flooded in: emails, messages, and urgent calls flashing incessantly. Each alert felt like a punch to the gut.

Rajeev entered cautiously, carrying two mugs of steaming coffee. He set one down in front of Aryan, pulling a chair close to him. "Aryan, have you slept at all?"

Aryan looked up with a wry smile. "Sleep? Right now, it feels like a luxury I can't afford."

Rajeev sighed, sipping his coffee. "You can't fight if you're exhausted. Trust me on this."

Aryan rubbed his temples, his frustration evident. "I keep replaying everything in my head, every internal email, every conversation we had. Where did we go wrong, Rajeev?"

Rajeev hesitated, then leaned forward earnestly. "I've rechecked everything. Our data was solid. Our intentions were right. But these leaks have been precisely chosen to look questionable."

Aryan looked sharply at Rajeev. "What does that mean?"

Rajeev paused before answering, as if carefully choosing his words. "Someone inside, someone we trusted, knew exactly what to pick," he said in a low voice. "They're distorting reality, making us look guilty."

Aryan stood up abruptly and began pacing the office. He stopped by the window, looking out over Bangalore's sprawling tech parks, the skyline now tinged with the muted orange of dawn. "If this is an inside job, Rajeev, the betrayal runs deeper than I ever imagined."

Rajeev watched him intently. "We'll figure it out. But right now, your priority is damage control."

Aryan turned sharply. "Damage control? You mean lie to the world?"

"No," Rajeev responded firmly. "I mean, tell our story clearly and truthfully. Stand behind what we built. People trust you, Aryan. Don't underestimate that."

Aryan was quiet for a moment. "And what if that trust is already broken?"

Rajeev met Aryan's gaze steadily. "Then you fight to earn it back."

Aryan considered Rajeev's words carefully, finally taking a deep, calming breath. "Alright," he said resolutely. "Let's do exactly that."

Rajeev smiled slightly, relieved. "Then let's start preparing for another detailed press conference."

***

Aryan entered the makeshift crisis room where key department heads were already gathered: compliance, PR, cybersecurity, and legal. The atmosphere in the room was heavy, the silence almost suffocating.

Sanjay stood up and motioned toward the screen behind him. "The media frenzy isn't slowing down. Every thirty minutes, another outlet is running fresh angles."

Aryan's voice was firm. "What are they saying now?"

Priya from PR clicked to the next slide. "They are reporting that the data logs from our oncology trials were tampered with, and that someone inside falsified results to match pilot targets. They're quoting 'sources close to TechNova' anonymous, of course."

Aryan's jaw tightened. "And investors?"

"They are jittery. Some have frozen funding. One VC firm just paused their second tranche," Sanjay said.

Aryan folded his arms, looking at the screen. "Who stands to gain from this?"

Rajeev leaned forward. "NeuroVista has a prototype. It is less accurate, less tested, but they've been eyeing our government contract for months. If we're out of the game…"

"…they walk in," Aryan finished the sentence, his eyes narrowing.

Sanjay nodded. "And they've got a clean PR sheet, unlike us right now."

Aryan turned to the cybersecurity head. "Any trace of the source of the leak?"

"It's encrypted, bounced off multiple nodes. But one IP resolved briefly from Whitefield, Bangalore. That narrows it down to a tech park zone."

Aryan stepped back, his mind spinning. "So it's someone local. Someone smart."

Priya added, "And someone who knows how to weaponize half-truths."

Aryan looked at Rajeev. "I want a timeline audit. It should include every person who had access to those pilot datasets: interns, consultants, everyone."

Rajeev nodded. "I'll have it by evening."

Sanjay hesitated. "And the media?" he asked. "What will be the tone for the press conference?"

Aryan's voice was cold as steel. "We don't get emotional," he said. "We stay clinical. We show them what Mediscan does and let the truth make the noise."

Around the room, department heads exchanged glances. Regardless of the noise outside, their loyalty to Aryan and TechNova remained unshaken.

There was a pause.

Then Priya asked, "What if they bring up the whistleblower?"

Aryan didn't blink. "We say we welcome transparency. We've got nothing to hide."

There was silence for a second. Then, one by one, the department heads nodded.

Aryan finally exhaled, quietly. "Let's clean the rot, all of it."

***

Rajeev entered Aryan's office without knocking. His face was tight, less composed than usual.

"Do you have a minute?" he asked, closing the door behind him.

Aryan looked up from his phone. "Barely. Investors are expecting me on a call in ten minutes."

"You might want to cancel that," Rajeev said, pulling up a tab on Aryan's desktop screen.

Aryan walked over to his desk. "What is it now?"

Rajeev clicked on a link. "This just dropped."

A grainy video began to play: Aryan, in a lab coat, speaking to a group of interns. The clip was edited, the words spliced. The caption read: *'We can always tweak results later. What matters is public confidence.'*

Aryan's face went pale. "That's fake! It's completely out of context."

He remembered that day clearly, how he had warned the interns about optimism bias and the importance of cross-verifying data, not about faking results.

"It doesn't matter," Rajeev said. "The damage is done. The clip's viral. It's trending on X. They've turned it into a meme."

Aryan's hands clenched the edge of the desk. "This is war. Someone wants to burn everything down."

"Whoever it is, they're two steps ahead. And worse, people are believing it. The narrative is shifting."

Aryan turned to the window. The skyline of Bangalore no longer looked inviting; it felt like a chessboard. "And we're the kings being cornered."

Rajeev hesitated, then said, "There's something else."

Aryan glanced back. "Go on."

"Anjali Kapoor from GlobalVision wants an exclusive. She claims to have sources inside TechNova. She's hinting she'll go public with a full exposé unless you speak first."

Aryan narrowed his eyes. "Is she bluffing?"

"She's good at what she does," Rajeev said. "She exposed the Horizon Biotech scandal last year. It took down their CEO."

Aryan was quiet for a long moment.

"Set up the interview," he said finally. "But it will be on my terms. There will be no live broadcast, no traps."

"Are you sure?" Rajeev asked. "This could backfire."

Aryan nodded slowly. "It's better I speak rather than let someone else write my story."

***

In his office, Aryan tapped open a locked folder on his phone. The screen filled with images, snapshots of past TechNova team events, photos from early Mediscan trials… and then one that made him stop.

Naina.

She was in the lab, arms crossed, laughing at something he'd said. The corner of Aryan's mouth twitched slightly at the memory.

He whispered to himself, "You always warned me to be careful with what I built."

There was a knock on the door.

Rajeev came in. "Sorry. I didn't mean to interrupt."

Aryan slipped the phone into his pocket. "What is it?"

Rajeev studied him for a second. "Are you okay?"

Aryan didn't answer immediately. "Do you remember Naina's first trial review?" he asked. "She flagged every possible ethical concern, even when we were just running projections."

Rajeev nodded. "She was cautious and intense. That's what made her so good."

Aryan's gaze drifted. "And I overrode her."

There was silence.

Rajeev stepped closer. "Aryan, the decision to scale Mediscan was on all of us. You didn't bury concerns; you addressed them."

"But did I rush it?" Aryan muttered. "Did I push too fast or too hard?"

Rajeev shook his head. "You built something revolutionary. That kind of innovation never comes clean."

Aryan looked up. "I keep thinking… if Naina were here, would she have warned me sooner? Would she have seen this unravelling before it began?"

Rajeev sighed. "Maybe. But she's not here, Aryan. You are. And we need you clear-headed, not chasing ghosts."

Aryan nodded slowly, his eyes distant. "It's not about chasing ghosts. It's about remembering what kept me human in the first place."

***

Back in his apartment, Aryan flipped slowly through the album, its pages heavy with memory. Photos from TechNova's founding days. R&D trials. Award ceremonies. Naina, smiling beside a whiteboard, caught mid-explanation.

His thumb rested on her face.

The room was silent, except for the occasional honk outside his window.

"You always hated the media," he said aloud, as if she were in the room. "You said truth didn't belong in ten-second sound-bites."

A voice interrupted him. Rajeev was standing at the door.

"You're not dressed yet," he said, stepping inside.

Aryan blinked. "Dressed for what?"

Rajeev raised an eyebrow. "The interview with Anjali. You're supposed to meet her in 45 minutes."

Aryan closed the album slowly. "It feels like I've already been interviewed by the world today."

Rajeev gave a dry smile. "This one, at least, you will control."

Aryan stood up, rubbing the back of his neck. "Do you think I should mention Naina?"

Rajeev paused before replying, "Only if it's true to what you feel. But don't make it a tribute; make it a reminder of your integrity."

Aryan looked at his reflection in the window. "She used to say integrity doesn't live in announcements; it lives in decisions."

Rajeev stepped closer to him. "Then make yours count tonight."

Aryan nodded slowly. "Help me draft the final points. I want every word to cut through the noise."

Rajeev smirked. "That's more like you."

Aryan walked to the mirror, straightening his collar. "Let's give them the Aryan Mehra they have forgotten."

The interview began under bright, clinical lights at Global Vision Studio. Aryan sat across from journalist Anjali Kapoor. The cameras were live.

Anjali: "Mr Mehra, thank you for joining us tonight. There's a lot of curiosity, but even more concern. Shall we begin?"

Aryan: *(nodding)* "Let's get to it."

Anjali: "First of all, do you deny the allegations that TechNova manipulated trial data for Mediscan?"

Aryan: "Absolutely. The core data was never manipulated. What's being circulated are selectively clipped internal conversations, distorted to imply corruption where there was none."

Anjali: "But some of those conversations show concern about performance gaps, don't they?"

Aryan: "Yes, because that's what responsible development is. We flagged issues, and we solved them. The whistleblower didn't expose a secret; they repackaged transparency to look like a cover-up."

Anjali: *(leaning forward)* "There's talk that you fast-tracked Mediscan to beat your rivals. That it was ambition, not ethics, behind your timeline."

Aryan: *(calmly)* "Innovation isn't a slow-motion parade, Anjali. We pushed because we had something that could save lives. We tested, reviewed, and peer-verified. We didn't cut corners; we made hard decisions."

Anjali: "But did your investors pressure you to push it faster?"

Aryan: "Investors are always watching the clock. But the final say was mine. I take full responsibility for the pace."

Anjali: "So you admit to being the sole driver behind the launch?"

Aryan: *(firmly)* "Yes. And I stand by the decision."

Anjali: "Your critics say Mediscan flagged too many false positives in early trials. They also claim it created panic in under-resourced clinics. What do you say to that?"

Aryan: "It's true that Mediscan caught anomalies others missed. In some cases, yes, it created an alarm. But in most of those cases, the follow-ups proved the AI was right. Early detection saves lives. Panic is a side effect of awareness, not negligence."

"In fact, last year in Chhattisgarh, Mediscan flagged early-stage tumours in five patients who showed no external symptoms. They are all now in successful recovery. Awareness saved them."

Anjali: "Do you believe your technology should continue being used during the investigation?"

Aryan: "If the alternative is letting people go undiagnosed, then yes. Mediscan doesn't deserve to be silenced for political comfort."

Anjali: *(softening slightly)* "How personal is this for you?"

Aryan: *(quietly)* "Very. I built this after watching someone close to me slip through the cracks of late diagnosis. I didn't create Mediscan to make headlines. I created it to stop that kind of pain from being repeated."

Anjali: "Do you mean Naina Rao?"

Aryan: *(a flicker in his eyes)* "Yes."

Anjali: "What would she have thought of this moment?"

Aryan: *(long pause)* "She would've demanded better from me. And from everyone trying to twist the truth right now."

Anjali: "One last question. If this storm takes everything from you: TechNova, Mediscan, your reputation, what remains?"

Aryan: *(looking into the camera)* "My truth. And the people who needed this tech yesterday and will still need it tomorrow. I believe truth takes its time, but it always arrives."

Anjali: *(nodding)* "Thank you, Mr Mehra."

The camera light faded. The room went still.

***

As Aryan stepped into TechNova's executive lounge, all eyes turned to him.

Rajeev was already checking his phone. "Your closing line is everywhere. It's trending under #TruthTakesItsTime."

Aryan sank into a chair. "That wasn't the plan. I was supposed to stay clinical."

"It worked because it wasn't rehearsed," said Priya, entering with her tablet. "We've had over fifty media mentions in the last hour. Some are negative, but a surprising number are also shifting tone."

Aryan looked up. "Shifting how?"

Priya scrolled through headlines: "'Mehra Faces Fire with Poise', 'Aryan Speaks, Markets Listen', and my favourite 'Tech CEO Dares the Storm'."

Rajeev smirked. "It sounds like they've finally remembered you're a human being."

Aryan raised an eyebrow. "Let's not celebrate too early. What about investors?"

Sanjay entered just then, phone pressed to his ear. He mouthed, "Give me a sec," then hung up and turned to the group. "That was our lead VC. They're holding for now. No withdrawal. But they want constant updates."

Aryan nodded. "We'll give them one every morning. And every evening, if needed."

He looked around the room, his people all still standing with him despite the storm. That meant something.

Priya tilted her head. "You do know what this means, don't you?"

"What?"

"You've become the story now, Aryan. Not Mediscan. You."

"Then I'd better control the next chapter," said Aryan, unfazed.

***

Rajeev walked into Aryan's study without knocking. "Aryan, something just came in."

Aryan looked up slowly. "What is it now?"

Rajeev held up his phone. "It's an anonymous drop. This time, it's not the media. It has been sent directly to the Central Health Ethics Board."

Aryan narrowed his eyes. "What does it say?"

"It says that Mediscan's machine learning module was allegedly reverse-engineered from an unreleased military project and also that you bypassed patent protocols."

Aryan said sharply, "That's complete fiction."

Rajeev nodded. "I know. But the details in the file... It's written by someone who knew our development pipeline. This isn't amateur slander."

Aryan clenched his jaw. "This leak isn't about ethics. It's a takedown. A full dismantling."

He paced the room, muttering to himself, "They're turning trust into suspicion, truth into liability."

Rajeev sat down. "This could trigger a full-blown investigation, not just on TechNova but on you, too."

Aryan stopped pacing. "That means they're not after just the company. They're after me."

A tense silence hung in the air.

Rajeev broke it. "What do we do?"

Aryan turned toward the wall where a framed quote from his father hung: "If they doubt your truth, let your actions be the evidence."

He took a deep breath. "We fight harder. And we prepare for the worst."

***

Aryan stood at the head of the table in TechNova's internal command room, hands resting on the glass surface. "Everyone in this room knows what's happening isn't normal."

Sanjay leaned forward. "We're under coordinated attack. It's not just a smear campaign; this is calculated, systemic."

Priya added, "And whoever's behind it has real, sensitive access. That narrows down the list."

Rajeev looked around. "Or it widens it, if we consider former employees, ex-consultants, even silent stakeholders."

Aryan nodded slowly. "We start tracing every thread. Background checks. Exit interviews. Anything odd in the last six months, we flag it."

Sanjay tapped the table. "We'll need authorization to access archived mail logs and NDA records."

"You have it," Aryan said without hesitation. "And double up on endpoint security. There should be no more leaks. From this moment, TechNova is on lockdown."

Rajeev raised a brow. "Lockdown? That'll draw attention."

Aryan met his gaze. "It's better we control the story than clean up another explosion."

Priya's phone buzzed. She glanced at the screen and frowned. "There's chatter online," she said. "Some insiders are anonymously claiming Mediscan flagged false positives to inflate success metrics."

Aryan clenched his fists. "They're seeding fear before regulators even step in."

Sanjay added, "Then we get ahead of the regulators. We need to submit our own audit to show we have nothing to hide."

Aryan nodded. "Do it. Voluntarily. Full transparency."

He looked around the room. "We've built something that saves lives. That doesn't vanish just because someone's afraid of what we've achieved."

The team nodded, silent but charged.

***

Aryan was in the office late at night. Everyone had left. He stood alone, staring out over the Bangalore skyline. His phone buzzed with another anonymous message.

He picked up the phone. The message read:

"Truth isn't what you say. It's what you hide. And you're hiding plenty, Mr Mehra."

He stared at the screen for a long moment. There was no sender's name. No trace.

Rajeev reappeared at the door, jacket slung over his shoulder. "I'm heading out. Are you coming?"

Aryan didn't turn around. "I'll stay a little longer."

Rajeev paused. "Are you okay?"

"Not yet," Aryan replied. "But I will be."

Rajeev nodded and left.

Aryan turned back to his desk and opened a locked drawer. Inside was a slim black notebook: Naina's old lab journal. He flipped through its pages, each filled with scribbled theories, ethical questions, and side notes in the margins.

He whispered, "You saw something. I just didn't listen."

He closed the journal, slid it into his coat pocket, and sat down at his desk. A new determination lit his eyes.

"You want war?" he murmured to the shadows. "Then I'll fight like someone with nothing left to lose."

Outside, the city of Bangalore pulsed with lights, unaware that its biggest tech storm had just begun.

***

Chapter 3

THE GATHERING STORM

Aryan stood by the window, overlooking Whitefield's gleaming tech towers as the Bangalore skyline stretched silently beyond the glass. Lights blinked like signals from a city that had already judged him.

On the muted TV, headlines scrolled relentlessly:

"TechNova CEO Under Fire"

"Whistleblower Links AI to Trafficking Network"

He turned away. The room felt colder than it was.

"They're not even pretending to wait for proof," he muttered.

Down below, traffic crawled along Whitefield Main Road, headlights blurring into long neon streams against the misty evening air.

Everyone had left: legal, PR, and even Rajeev. He was alone. And not just in the building.

He stared at the photo on the shelf of TechNova's founding team, all smiles and dreams. His eyes paused on one face.

Kabir.

"You once told me to call before the world eats me alive," Aryan murmured.

He picked up his phone and scrolled through old contacts.

Kabir. His number was still saved under "Chaos with a Keyboard".

He hesitated, thumb hovering. Then he hit 'Call'.

"Look who finally remembered I exist," Kabir's voice came through, playful and sharp as ever.

Aryan exhaled, almost smiling. "I need your help."

"Is it that bad?"

"It's worse," Aryan said. "Someone's hacking our systems. Leaking files. They've turned the media against me. It's coordinated."

There was a pause.

"You're not just being paranoid, are you?" Kabir asked.

"There's a pattern of timed drops, selective files, even internal memos twisted to look criminal."

Kabir's tone shifted. "Okay. You've got my attention."

"I need you to trace the leaks," Aryan said. "Find out how they got in and who's behind it."

"What about access?"

"I'll send credentials tonight. And a folder of the flagged files."

Kabir chuckled. "You realize this is illegal, don't you?"

"I'm aware of that."

"Alright," Kabir said. "But if I find something big, I get naming rights for the operation."

Aryan managed a tired smile. "It's a deal."

"Sit tight, Mr Mehra. If someone's playing God in your system, I'll smoke them out."

Aryan ended the call and stared at his phone.

Help was on the way, but so was war.

***

Aryan didn't move for a long time. He stared at the dark screen, thumb hovering for a second longer over another name.

Naina.

The silence in the room deepened. Her name carried weight, even now. Especially now.

He opened her contact, then closed it.

"Is it too soon… or too late?" he murmured.

They hadn't spoken since she walked out of TechNova. The fallout had been personal, professional, and painful. But if anyone could read between the lines of this setup, it was her.

He stood and paced slowly. The media was spinning half-truths into monsters. Kabir could track the leak, but Naina could tell him why it was happening. He stopped pacing and looked out the window again. The city buzzed in the distance. He remembered late nights in the lab with her, debating ethics, tearing apart systems, and building trust.

He pulled out his phone again. Naina's name stared back at him.

No more debating. He hit 'Call'. The line rang. Once. Twice. Then the call was picked up.

"Hello?" Her voice was exactly as he remembered it; clear, sharp, unreadable.

Aryan hesitated. "It's me."

A pause.

Then Naina said dryly, "It took you long enough. I thought I'd never hear from you again."

"I didn't think I had the right to call you," Aryan replied quietly.

She let that hang. "So... why did you call now?"

"There's something wrong. It's bigger than me. Bigger than TechNova."

"You have finally figured that out, huh?" she said, her voice dry.

"I'm not calling to fix us, Naina. I need your eyes and your mind."

She exhaled. "What is it?"

"There's a campaign; targeted, timed, surgical. Internal files have been twisted, taken out of context. Now I'm being linked to trafficking cases, all based on half-truths."

She was silent. Then she said, "That's not just sabotage; it's strategic character assassination."

Aryan's voice lowered. "Exactly. I think someone inside helped make it possible."

"And you want me to dive into your mess? Why me?"

"Because you're the only one who ever told me the truth, even when I didn't want to hear it."

Another pause.

"Where do I begin?" she asked finally.

"You tell me."

She sighed. "Send me everything: timeline, leaks, any names you suspect."

"I will."

"But I'm not doing this for you," she added. "I'm doing it for the people who might get hurt if this goes unchecked."

"I wouldn't expect anything less," Aryan said.

For the first time in days, something inside him steadied.

"You still don't sound like a man who's telling me everything," Naina said.

Aryan leaned back in his chair. "Because I'm still connecting the dots."

"I don't work on guesses," she replied. "Give me facts."

"I've already got Kabir tracing the source of the leaks."

That caught her off-guard. "Kabir? Hacker Kabir?"

"The same. He's working on the backend. I need you on motive and pattern."

"I see. And what's your theory?"

Aryan paused before replying, "Whoever's behind this knows Mediscan inside out. They've timed the leaks to coincide with major milestones, investor meets, government reviews, and media cycles."

Naina's tone sharpened. "It sounds like someone who used to be inside."

"Or still is."

She was quiet for a moment. "Has anyone been behaving... unusually? Changed departments or taken unexplained leaves?"

"Rajeev mentioned a few resignations over the last quarter. They were mostly analysts. We didn't think much of it at the time."

"Get me details of their names, dates, and roles."

"I'll have Kabir pull HR logs."

"And Aryan?"

"Yes?"

"Don't sugarcoat anything. If you want me involved, you have to give me the full picture, even the ugly parts."

He nodded, though she couldn't see it. "I will."

"Alright," she said. "Now hang up the phone and start compiling. I want everything by tonight."

Aryan smiled faintly. "You are bossy as ever."

"And you're still lucky I picked up your call," she replied, then disconnected the line.

Aryan stared at the screen.

This was happening. Naina was in.

Somewhere beyond the clattering loops of Outer Ring Road, Naina would already be analyzing the fragments he'd sent, her mind cutting through lies where others saw only noise.

***

Aryan tapped his phone against his palm, staring at the call log with Naina's name still glowing.

He whispered to himself, "She said yes. That's all that matters."

Just then, a new message pinged.

Kabir: "Sent a tracker script. Install it into TechNova's mail server logs. Let's see who's been playing games."

Aryan opened his laptop, decrypting Kabir's file. The interface was slick, clean code, and silent operation.

He dialled Kabir's number. "I've got it and am uploading it now."

"Good," Kabir replied. "Also, I went through last week's firewall logs and found something weird."

"Weird how?"

"Someone accessed archived QA reports using a dummy admin profile, 'SystemRun99'. And it routed through a proxy in Goa. One of the proxy pings had even bounced off a public Wi-Fi node from Phoenix Marketcity Mall, the perfect cover in tech-saturated Whitefield."

Aryan frowned. "We don't have any servers in Goa."

"Exactly. It's either a planted trail, or someone got sloppy."

Aryan's jaw tightened. "Can you trace the origin?"

Kabir chuckled. "Already on it. But I need a list of employees who had access to internal audit folders."

"I'm forwarding the HR access log now," Aryan said.

"Okay. Also, tell your friend, Naina, she still owes me a coffee."

Aryan blinked. "You knew I called her?"

"Of course. I read your silences like subtitles."

Aryan shook his head, a half-laugh escaping. "You never change."

"And neither do your enemies. Keep your guard up, Aryan. This rabbit hole's about to get deep."

Aryan stared at the blinking cursor on his screen as Kabir's words echoed in his mind. He opened the archived QA reports Kabir had flagged. Most of the data looked untouched, but one file had been edited two days ago. The timestamp didn't match any internal activity logs.

His phone buzzed again with a message.

Naina: "Just reviewed the media leak timelines. The releases aren't random. They sync with internal review deadlines and external audits. Someone's playing chess."

Aryan typed back quickly: "Kabir found unauthorized logins. Goa proxy server. Digging deeper."

Naina: "I want to cross-check everything. I'll start with the first Mediscan pilot case. The hospital in Mysuru. Can you get me the original reports?"

He hesitated, then typed: "Some of them are sealed under our NDA protocols."

Her response came fast.

Naina: "Then unseal them. You called me, don't hold back now."

Aryan sighed and typed back: "You'll have them tonight." He leaned back, staring at the glow of the screen.

The investigation wasn't just alive, it was accelerating. But the closer they got, the more dangerous it felt.

He opened another file. This one had Naina's initials in one of her old review reports. She'd warned of inconsistencies in data tagging back then, but he hadn't listened to her.

Now, that warning might be the key to everything.

***

Naina sat on her bed, her laptop glowing in the dark. Dozens of windows were open on it: hospital records, old QA logs, and encrypted PDFs Aryan had just sent.

She muttered, "You were always brilliant, Aryan. But you never looked close enough."

She clicked open the report on the Mysuru pilot case:

Initial results: promising

Follow-up entries: missing

Audit comments: redacted

She frowned.

Just then, her phone buzzed.

Aryan: "Sent everything. Let me know if anything feels off."

She typed back: "It already does. Why are the patient follow-up entries blanked out?"

Aryan: "They were flagged in a legacy QA sweep. That database was archived after we shifted platforms. You think it's connected?"

Naina: "Too early to say. But blank spaces in a medical trial aren't random; they're erasures."

She leaned closer to the screen, scrolling through email trails attached to the report. One subject line stood out:

"RE: Case #4578 anomaly – advised internal flag, no external disclosure."

Her eyebrows lifted, and she clicked it open. The text was limited to just a single sentence:

"Keep it internal. Let Aryan focus on launch timelines."

Naina sat back, lips pressed in a tight line. "They didn't just hide things from regulators," she said aloud. "They hid it from him, too." Her jaw clenched. "Now I want to know who sent this."

Naina's call came through just as Aryan was compiling another data folder.

He picked up. "Did you find something?"

"Yes," she said, voice clipped. "Something you should've seen years ago."

Aryan's stomach tightened. "Go on."

"There's an internal email about Case #4578, an anomaly in the Mysuru pilot. Someone advised your team to keep it quiet."

"I never saw that," Aryan said. "I swear."

Naina didn't let up. "Then someone close to you made sure of that. The message clearly says, 'Let Aryan focus on launch timelines.' That's not random phrasing."

Aryan ran a hand over his face, then asked, "Who was copied?"

"There are only two names, Bhaskar Deshmukh and Devika Rao."

Aryan blinked. "Devika? She was head of QA back then."

"And now she's at NeuroVista," Naina snapped. "Your biggest competitor."

Aryan stood up slowly. "No… no, she said she left on ethical grounds,"

"Maybe she did. Or maybe she took your tech and cleaned her hands on the way out."

There was a long silence.

Finally, Aryan said, "This was under my nose the whole time."

Naina's voice softened. "You trusted the wrong people. Now we will fix it."

Aryan nodded, though his voice cracked. "Then let's burn the whole lie down."

"You start with Bhaskar," Naina said. "He's still in TechNova. That makes him the most dangerous piece on the board."

***

Aryan didn't wait. He stormed into the office the next morning before anyone else had arrived. The glass corridors of TechNova were quiet, still recovering from the week's chaos. He found Bhaskar at his desk, sipping coffee, looking unruffled.

"Good morning, sir," Bhaskar said, half standing up.

"Sit," Aryan said flatly. "We need to talk."

Bhaskar's smile faltered. "Is everything alright?"

Aryan dropped a file on his desk. "Case #4578. Does that ring a bell?"

Bhaskar glanced at the file, then forced a frown. "That was years ago. QA flagged an inconsistency, which was resolved."

"Resolved? Or buried?"

Bhaskar opened his mouth, but Aryan cut in. "Why wasn't I copied on that mail? Why was Devika the only other person in the loop?"

Bhaskar shifted in his chair and said, "You were dealing with the stress of the launch. We made a judgement call."

Aryan stepped closer. "You made a call to hide flagged results in a pilot meant to save lives."

Bhaskar held up his hands as if in defence. "I didn't erase anything," he said. "Devika handled the follow-up."

"She's with NeuroVista now."

There was silence as the room filled with the gravity of what Aryan had said.

Aryan's voice dropped. "You fed them our system's vulnerabilities, didn't you?"

Bhaskar paled. "I... I needed leverage in case things went south."

Aryan stared him down. "You used Mediscan as leverage?"

"I didn't leak it to the media."

"But you opened the gate," Aryan said coldly.

He turned and walked out of the room.

Bhaskar sat frozen, sweat forming at his temples.

Back in his office, Aryan shut the door and leaned against it. His hands trembled slightly, not with fear, but anger. Bhaskar was a man he'd mentored and trusted with sensitive review cycles. He was someone who had smiled in every board meeting... had quietly played a double game.

Aryan slumped into his chair, staring blankly at the wall. "How many more are there?" he muttered.

The intercom buzzed. It was Rajeev. "Boss, is everything okay? Bhaskar looked like he'd seen a ghost."

Aryan hesitated, then said, "Come in."

Rajeev entered cautiously. "You look worse today."

Aryan sighed. "Bhaskar admitted to sitting on key QA anomalies during our pilot phase."

Rajeev's eyes widened. "What? Why?"

"He wanted to leverage a safety net if the company turned on him."

Rajeev shook his head. "Jesus! That's... low."

Aryan looked at him. "How many more are still hiding behind polished decks and fake smiles?"

Rajeev didn't answer.

Aryan continued, "Devika's with NeuroVista. Bhaskar helped shield her back then. Now, we're bleeding trust because of it."

Rajeev lowered his voice and asked, "Should we take this to legal?"

"Not yet," Aryan said. "If we go public, we'll trigger panic. Investors will bail. I want to finish this internally first."

Rajeev nodded slowly. "So what do you need?"

Aryan looked up at him and said, "Help me build a list of anyone who had access to early Mediscan datasets and suddenly left or changed departments. Let's map the fault lines."

By noon, Aryan's office looked like a war room. Sticky notes, printed emails, and access logs covered the glass board. Rajeev stood at one end, flipping through a thick file. "Kabir just pinged," he said. "He's isolated three users who accessed the archived Mediscan QA files in the past two months outside of protocol."

Aryan circled names with a marker. "Who are they?"

"They include one intern who left in April, one current DevOps fellow, and one wildcard, Anand Chauhan. He is a former consultant who was let go after budget cuts."

Aryan paused. "I remember Anand. He was quiet, technical, and always kept to himself."

"In other words, exactly the type people forget but who see everything," Rajeev said.

Aryan nodded. "Where is he now?"

"Last we heard, he was freelancing for small AI labs. Kabir's checking his IP trails."

Aryan turned to the board. "These aren't isolated cases. There's a pattern. Strategic silence. Carefully timed departures."

Rajeev looked up. "Do you think this was planned from the inside?"

Aryan stared at the red dots now connecting across the board. "I think this conspiracy didn't start outside TechNova; it was born right here, in glass offices, behind our backs."

Just then, another alert popped up on Aryan's screen.

Naina: "Just finished correlating the pilot inconsistencies with Bhaskar's review window. You were played. Hard."

Aryan whispered, almost to himself, "Not anymore."

***

As Aryan walked down the glass corridors toward the boardroom, the muted roar of traffic from Old Madras Road seeped faintly through the high-rise walls, a reminder that outside TechNova's glass fortress, life rolled on, unaffected by the war brewing inside.

Aryan stood in front of the centre of the glass board, marker in hand. The patterns were becoming harder to ignore.

He drew a red line from Anand Chauhan's name to NeuroVista.

Rajeev asked, "Do you think he's the bridge?"

Aryan nodded. "He was Devika's contract lead during the early neural engine development. They worked closely. Too closely."

Rajeev crossed his arms. "Do you think they passed proprietary algorithms?"

"If not the full engine, then at least its skeleton," Aryan said. "Enough to recreate."

He turned to his laptop and started typing rapidly. "I'm drafting a private brief to the legal team," he said. "Confidential. No external flags yet."

Rajeev said quietly, "Once this breaks, Aryan… there's no undoing it."

Aryan looked up. "It's already broken. Now we control how it ends."

Rajeev walked closer. "And if Devika denies everything?"

"She will," Aryan said. "But we don't need a confession; we need patterns, proof, and motive. Then we present the entire story at once, not in pieces."

Rajeev nodded. "What about Bhaskar?"

"He's already folded. I want him watched discreetly."

Aryan's phone buzzed again.

Kabir: "Anand's email just pinged a new outbound file dump. It's big."

Aryan muttered, "They're still covering tracks."

He looked at Rajeev. "Get Kabir to trace where that file's going," he said. "I want to know who's pulling the strings and sand who they answer to."

Kabir called instead of texting this time. His voice was sharper than usual. "Aryan, we've got a problem."

Aryan stepped out of the boardroom. "What is it now?"

"The file Anand sent out didn't just contain internal QA reports; it had fragments of Mediscan's core learning model. Someone patched it together, and it's being uploaded on the dark web."

Aryan's heart skipped. "How long until it goes live?"

"Maybe hours. Maybe less. It's being seeded fast. Torrent-based."

Rajeev, listening beside him, swore under his breath.

Aryan asked, "Can you kill it?"

Kabir exhaled. "I'm trying, but once it scatters to enough nodes, even I can't pull it back."

Aryan clenched his jaw. "Who's downloading it?"

"Mostly offshore nodes, but a few Indian domains, too, private AI labs, some university proxies."

Aryan rubbed his face. "They're not just trying to ruin me; they want to erase the origin of Mediscan, make it public property."

Rajeev said, "That's theft, strategic and irreversible."

Kabir added, "This isn't just a leak anymore; it is a digital hijack."

Aryan's voice was cold. "Then we hit back. Not just with words but with data, dates, code snapshots, proof of every stolen line and every traitor."

He turned to Rajeev. "Get the team ready. Tomorrow, we go public."

Rajeev asked, "On all of it?"

Aryan nodded. "Everything."

***

Late at night, Aryan sat alone in his office. The building had gone quiet, but his thoughts hadn't.

A single desk lamp lit the stack of files in front of him: timelines, access logs, QA trails, and the names of those who'd once called themselves loyal.

His phone buzzed.

Naina: "Got the report drafts. I'm cleaning up the language, making it airtight. Don't hold back tomorrow."

Aryan replied: "I won't."

He stared at the framed quote on his wall that his father had left him: "Truth isn't always loud. But it never stays buried."

Aryan stood up and walked to the window. Below, Bangalore hummed like any other night, but up here, a war was about to begin, not for survival, but for truth. He took a deep breath. No more second-guessing. No more protecting reputations. No more playing nice with people who'd sold out integrity for convenience. He turned off the lamp, leaving only the city lights behind him.

"Tomorrow," he said to himself, "we don't defend; we expose."

He left the office without looking back.

***

Chapter 4

SHADOWS OF BETRAYAL

The door to the hotel suite clicked open, and Naina stepped inside without hesitation.

Aryan stood near the window, one hand in his pocket, the other holding a cup of untouched coffee. He turned when he heard the door open.

"You're early," he said, voice calm but uncertain.

"I'm punctual," she replied, looking around the room. Her eyes didn't linger on him.

Aryan, too, avoided meeting her gaze for longer than a heartbeat. The past was too raw, the stakes too high.

He gestured toward the armchair. "Please have a seat."

"I'll stand," she said. "Let's not pretend this is casual."

Aryan set the cup down. "Right. Straight to business."

She finally looked at him, her eyes cool. "That's what you called me for, isn't it?"

He nodded slowly. "Yes. But… thank you for coming."

"You sounded desperate," she said flatly. "I was curious to see what that looks like on you."

A faint smile tugged at his lips, but he didn't answer.

She walked to the table, dropped her bag on it, and pulled out a folder. "Before we begin, there are a few rules."

He raised an eyebrow. "Rules?"

"There will be no emotional detours, no trips down memory lane, and no guilt plays. We focus on the case. Nothing else."

Aryan gave a small nod. "Understood."

There was a pause. The air between them was sharp, fragile.

Then Naina added, more quietly, "And don't try to impress me. It won't work."

Aryan met her gaze. "That's not why I called you."

For a moment, neither of them moved.

And just like that, the investigation was underway.

Naina flipped open the folder she'd brought and began spreading documents across the table.

Aryan took a cautious step closer. "You've already started digging?"

She didn't look up. "I started the moment I agreed to meet you."

He watched her scan a page, highlighter in hand. "You're still thorough."

"I am still two steps ahead," she corrected, then paused. "Your turn."

Aryan moved toward his laptop. "Kabir traced the original leak back to an access log tied to Bhaskar Deshmukh."

Her head jerked up. "Bhaskar? He was your compliance fellow, wasn't he?"

"He was also one of the few with unrestricted QA access," said Aryan.

Naina leaned back, her arms crossed. "That's too convenient. People like Bhaskar don't move unless someone tells them to."

Aryan frowned. "Do you think he's covering for someone?"

"I think he's the front, not the face."

She handed him a document. "This is a trace log from a deleted access point in your internal QA server," she explained. "The metadata's been wiped, but the timestamp overlaps perfectly with the day of the Mysuru pilot redaction."

Aryan blinked. "Where did you get this?"

"I never deleted my mirror logs," she said. "Unlike some people, I plan for betrayal."

He stared at the printout. "This proves someone manipulated the data before the pilot launch."

Naina's voice was quiet but firm. "It was someone close, with authority."

Aryan looked up at her. "So it wasn't just sabotage; it was strategy."

She nodded once and said, "Welcome to your real problem."

***

Aryan slid the document closer, eyes scanning the data trail Naina had brought.

"This was before we even finalized the pilot," he murmured.

Naina didn't look up. "Exactly. This means someone had intent long before the public ever saw Mediscan."

He leaned back in his chair. "Why didn't anyone flag this?"

"They did," she replied. "You just didn't listen to them."

Her words landed like a slap. Aryan stiffened.

"I didn't ignore warnings," he said quietly. "I trusted my team."

"You trusted loyalty more than logic," she shot back. "And now you're cleaning up the mess."

He looked at her, jaw tight. "Are you here to blame me or fix this?"

She met his gaze. "I'm here to fix it, but we won't get far if you keep defending ghosts."

Aryan turned back to the file. "There were moments I doubted, but the board wanted the launch. The investors…"

She cut him off. "Don't tell me what the board wanted. Tell me what you knew and didn't say."

There was a long silence.

Then Aryan spoke, slower now. "I knew someone had tampered with the QA pipeline, but we couldn't trace it. And Bhaskar swore it was a server error."

"And you believed him."

"I wanted to."

Naina's voice softened, almost imperceptibly. "That's what scares me the most."

Aryan looked at her, words stuck in his throat.

She returned to the documents. "Let's move on," she said matter-of-factly. "The past won't help unless you finally admit it broke you."

She reached into her bag and pulled out a silver flash drive, placing it on the table between them.

Aryan raised an eyebrow. "What's that?"

"Your blind spot," she replied. "Run it."

He hesitated. "You trust me with it?"

She gave a faint smile. "It's encrypted. You can't read it without my code."

He inserted it into his laptop. A window popped up, locked tight.

"What am I looking at?" he asked.

"It's an access trace, compiled from mirrored server logs that your IT team buried."

Aryan's jaw tightened. "Have you had this all along?"

"I've been updating it since yesterday. And what I found points in one direction."

She leaned forward. "The user tag that keeps popping up—ADM-VK97. Do you know who that belongs to?"

He stared at her, the letters sinking in. "Vikram Sharma?"

Naina nodded. "Your former project head, the one who left mid-phase during the Mediscan pilot."

Aryan blinked. "That's impossible. He was removed from the system."

"Clearly not."

Aryan clenched his fists. "I hadn't heard his name in years."

"Well, his digital footprints are all over the data manipulation logs."

Aryan sat back, stunned.

"Either someone used his credentials," she said, "or Vikram never really left."

"He was there when it started," Aryan said in a low voice.

Naina leaned in. "Maybe he's still here, just hiding better than you imagined."

Aryan stared at the flash drive still plugged into his laptop. His fingers hovered over the keyboard, but his mind was clearly elsewhere.

Naina watched him. "Say it," she said.

He blinked. "Say what?"

"What are you thinking. Don't edit it for me."

He hesitated. "I just... I trusted Vikram. He was intense, brilliant. And loyal. At least, I thought so."

Naina folded her arms. "People don't always leave with clean exits. Sometimes they leave pieces behind or take a few with them."

Aryan looked at her. "Is that what you think I did?"

She held his gaze. "No. But I think you looked away when you shouldn't have."

He nodded slowly. "You're not wrong."

She moved closer to the screen. "Scroll down. There's a log entry time-stamped three days before Vikram resigned."

Aryan scrolled, eyes narrowing. "He accessed the diagnostic API layer."

Naina nodded. "That was not part of his job scope at that point, but no one stopped him."

Aryan rubbed his temple. "We were in the middle of a funding round," he said. "Everyone was stretched."

"You let things slip," she said, not accusing, just stating a fact.

He looked up at her. "And you didn't?"

Naina's smile was faint and bittersweet. "That's why I left," she said. "I knew I was about to."

For a moment, neither of them spoke.

Then Aryan said, "Maybe this was never about the product. Maybe it was about us not watching each other closely enough."

She didn't reply, but she didn't argue either. Aryan turned back to the screen, his gaze sharpened, "On Vikram's last day, he logged in from a remote IP outside the TechNova firewall."

Naina leaned in. "That's the session that triggered the original pipeline rewrite. Do you see the timestamp?"

Aryan nodded. "Two-forty AM. The building was locked. Only server access."

She added, "And after that, there's no activity. Nothing. Just a clean exit."

He frowned. "That's not how a resignation trail looks," he said. "Someone wipes a record like that when they don't want questions."

Aryan opened a background search on Vikram's ID, checking archived HR logs. "He listed 'personal burnout' as the reason for his resignation and requested a silent separation."

Naina scoffed. "Burnout doesn't lead to surgical log wipes. This was calculated."

Aryan stared at the date again and said thoughtfully, “That was the same week we started presenting to the Ministry of Health.”

“It was the perfect time to pull a fast one, sneak it in while all eyes were elsewhere,” Naina said.

He rubbed his forehead. “He had access to our original prediction model. If he altered it, it would explain the false-positive spikes in the pilot.”

Naina’s tone hardened. “And the reputational collapse that followed.”

Aryan looked at her. “What do you want to do?”

She didn’t hesitate. “We find him.”

Aryan raised an eyebrow. “Do you really think he’s still in Bangalore?”

“No,” she replied. “I think he’s where your guilt hasn’t dared to go yet.”

***

“I still remember the day Vikram left,” Aryan said, leaning back. “He was calm and said he needed space, no drama.”

Naina raised an eyebrow. “That’s not the version I remember.”

Aryan frowned. “What do you mean?” he asked.

“I saw him two days before his resignation. He was furious and accused you of cutting corners. He said you were selling vision over truth.”

Aryan looked genuinely stunned. “He never said that to me.”

“Maybe he didn’t think it mattered anymore.”

Aryan crossed his arms. “He was under pressure like all of us. We had deadlines, investor demands…”

“And he thought you were compromising integrity,” she cut in. “That’s why he pulled back.”

Aryan shook his head. “We were pushing boundaries, not breaking them,” he defended. “That’s what innovation looks like.”

Naina replied softly, “Sometimes it’s hard to tell the difference when you’re the one holding the match.”

A tense silence settled between them.

Then Aryan asked, "Why didn't you tell me this back then?"

"I tried," she said. "But you'd already started building your castle, and no one questions the architect when the walls are still going up."

He said nothing, but cursed himself inwardly, not for trusting others, but for believing his vision alone could outrun their flaws. Naina stood up and walked toward the window. "You keep looking for betrayal in their hands, Aryan," she said. "Maybe you should start with your blind spots."

Aryan looked at her back, his expression unreadable. For once, he didn't defend himself. His phone buzzed, interrupting the silence. It was Kabir. Aryan answered on speaker. "Have you got something?"

Kabir's voice came fast, clipped. "Yes, you're going to want to sit for this."

Naina leaned in and said, "We're listening."

"I traced the server instance used by that ADM-VK97 ID. It was accessed again last night."

Aryan stood up quickly. "By who?"

"That's the thing. It was routed through a masked IP, but the data funnel led to a private cloud bucket hosted under a corporate alias."

"Which alias?" Naina asked.

Kabir paused, then said, "Arkaris Healthcare Solutions."

Naina's eyes widened. "That company went dormant three years ago."

Kabir added, "They reopened under a proxy director six months back. Can you guess where it's registered?"

"Noida," Aryan muttered.

"Bingo! And the access code used to trigger the transfer was old, really old. It was something embedded deep in the original Mediscan model, before your upgrade cycle."

Aryan's breath caught. "That would only be on two machines."

"Exactly," Kabir said. "Yours and Vikram's."

Silence fell.

Then Naina said, "He's not just covering his tracks; he's using the old shell company to push data out."

Kabir sighed. "And whatever he's doing with it is moving fast."

Aryan clenched his jaw. "Send me everything: logs, routing trail, proxy IDs."

Kabir said, "They're already in your inbox. And Aryan? You're officially being outplayed."

Aryan ended the call.

Naina looked at him. "Do you still think this is just sabotage?"

He didn't answer. Because he no longer did.

***

Aryan dropped his phone onto the table, his eyes dark with fury.

"He's been in our system for months," he muttered. "Under our nose. Using our past."

Naina remained calm. "That's the part that scares you the most, isn't it?" she asked. "That he used your own code, your own legacy against you."

Aryan paced the room. "I built Mediscan to help people, to find what others missed. And now it's being weaponized?"

Naina replied softly, "That's what happens when we build without guardrails."

He turned on her. "You think this is all my fault, don't you?"

She didn't flinch. "I think you're finally realizing that genius without accountability is a loaded gun."

He stopped pacing. "Why didn't I see this coming?"

"Because you trusted loyalty over caution," she said. "You thought your vision would protect you from betrayal."

Aryan's shoulders sagged. "I thought we were building something that couldn't be twisted."

"Well," she said, stepping closer, "you were wrong. Now the question is, are you going to keep blaming yourself, or are you going to fight back?"

He looked up, jaw clenched.

"I'm done blaming," he said. "But I'm not forgiving either."

"Good," Naina replied. "Then we might just be ready."

Aryan smiled bitterly, "It took losing everything to wake up."

She studied him for a moment, then said, "Maybe now you'll finally see what was always in the blind spot."

The sun had started its descent by the time Aryan and Naina left the TechNova campus. Traffic crawled past glass buildings and metro pillars, casting long shadows over the streets of Whitefield, the city's sprawling tech corridor.

Aryan drove in silence while Naina stared out the window, her arms folded but her mind clearly not idle.

Finally, she said, "Did you ever think it was all too perfect?"

"What?"

"TechNova. The clean image, the ethical speeches, the award nights. Like it was curated for a movie."

Aryan glanced at her. "So you think I was performing?"

She turned to him. "I think you believed it. That's what made it dangerous."

He didn't answer right away. The signal turned green, and the car rolled forward.

"I built it to be clean," he said. "But somewhere, someone got in and infected the code."

Naina's tone softened. "Then we debug it."

They pulled into a shaded bypass near the outskirts of Whitefield, merging onto an older road that twisted past abandoned warehouses and half-constructed buildings.

Aryan glanced at her and asked curiously, "How do you always know where to look?"

She smiled faintly. "Because I'm not the one who believes in perfect things."

They parked in front of a gate with a rusted sign, reading 'Unit 6B', barely hanging from a hook.

Aryan turned off the engine. "We're here."

She stepped out, holding her bag, and said, "Let's see what the perfect empire was built on."

***

Aryan sat down, fingers locked, elbows on the edge of the table.

For once, the room wasn't buzzing with data or accusations. Just silence.

Naina stood near the window, arms crossed. The night outside blinked with indifferent city lights.

"I never imagined it would come to this," Aryan said quietly.

She didn't turn. "You mean losing everything?"

"No," he replied. "Needing you to save it."

She exhaled. "You don't need me to save anything, Aryan. You need me to tell you the truth without sugarcoating it."

He looked at her. "You always did," he said quietly. "That's why it hurt so much when you left."

Naina finally faced him. "I didn't leave because I stopped believing in the product. I left because I stopped believing in you."

Aryan didn't flinch. "I know."

They stood in that space for a moment, past and present colliding in the stillness.

Then she added in a softer voice, "You were chasing brilliance, but you stopped looking at the cracks."

"I see them now," he said.

"Good," she replied. "Because brilliance doesn't matter if it's built on silence."

Aryan stood up slowly. "Thank you... for not walking away this time."

Naina shrugged. "I'm not here for you, Aryan. I'm here because the lie is bigger than both of us."

He nodded. "Then let's expose it together."

And for the first time that day, they both meant it.

Aryan leaned against the edge of the desk, his voice quieter now. "I've replayed our last conversation a hundred times in my mind."

Naina didn't respond right away. She was watching the city lights again, arms still folded, but her shoulders had drooped.

"I didn't know what to say back then," he continued. "You said I was losing myself, that TechNova was eating the parts of me that used to care."

She glanced over at him. "And you told me I was weak for walking away."

He sighed. "I was angry and afraid," he said. "You were the one person who challenged me without needing anything in return."

Naina turned fully to face him. "I didn't leave because you failed. I left because you stopped listening."

Aryan nodded slowly. "I didn't just lose a colleague; I lost my compass."

There was a pause.

Then she said in a quiet voice, "You stopped being Aryan Mehra, the builder. You became Aryan Mehra, the brand."

That line cut deeper than she probably meant it to.

Aryan swallowed. "Maybe I needed to fall for the truth to stick," he said bitterly.

Naina held his gaze. "You didn't need to fall; you needed to stop climbing things that were hollow."

The silence between them wasn't cold this time. It felt earned.

Aryan asked, "If we survive this... if we fix it, what then?"

Naina blinked, then smiled faintly. "Let's not get poetic," she replied. "We've got a shell company to visit."

He smiled back, just slightly. "Right. War first, philosophy later."

Aryan's phone buzzed again, this time, not a call, but a secure file transfer from Kabir.

He opened it.

Subject: Vikram's Digital Signature – Foreign IP Match

A red notification blinked at the bottom:

"Routing location: Prague, Czech Republic. Confirmed."

Aryan blinked. "He's abroad?"

Naina stepped closer, reading over his shoulder. "Prague?"

"There's a pattern here," Aryan murmured. "Why route it that far unless he's selling something bigger?"

Naina clicked through the next file Kabir had attached, a heatmap of data movement. Dots blinked from Bangalore to Noida… then Prague.

"Encrypted AI modules, biometric identifiers, patient prediction logs, he's distributing the core of Mediscan to offshore buyers," she said. Aryan clenched his jaw. "This isn't a leak. It's a black-market operation."

They weren't just stealing code, Aryan thought bitterly. They were auctioning pieces of lives, dreams, and trust.

Naina looked at him. "And now it has international implications," she said quietly.

They both turned as another file dropped into the inbox. Kabir's voice message:

"Aryan. Naina. He's not alone. I found other accounts linked to his activity... dummy vendors, stolen patents, and even ghost clinical trials. This fellow built an empire in your shadow."

Aryan muttered, "All using what we built to save lives."

Naina's voice dropped. "He's turned Mediscan into a currency. And someone's paying."

Aryan stepped back from the table. "Then we're not just exposing a fraud."

"We're cracking open a global network," she completed.

They looked at each other. "And we start tonight," he said.

***

The car sliced through the late-night silence, headlights sweeping over empty Bangalore roads. Aryan drove, his eyes on the road and hands tight on the wheel.

Naina sat beside him, laptop open, still scanning Kabir's last data trail.

"The coordinates match the Arkaris office park on Outer Ring Road," she said. "It's registered under a dead leasing company, no signage, no website."

"Which makes it the perfect drop site," Aryan muttered.

Naina glanced at him. "We should've brought someone with us."

"There's no time," he replied. "By morning, everything could be wiped."

She shut the laptop. "Do you have a plan?"

"Walk in. Watch. Document. No confrontations."

She raised an eyebrow. "Have you ever known a plan to go that smoothly?"

He allowed a tight smile. "Not once."

They turned into the quiet Bommasandra Industrial Zone; rows of warehouses, dark offices, forgotten parking lots. Aryan slowed as they approached a gated complex.

"There," Naina pointed. "Unit 6 B. The lights are on."

He pulled over and turned off the engine.

For a moment, they sat in silence.

"Last chance to turn back," Aryan said.

Naina replied without missing a beat, "You don't bring a firestarter if you want to walk away."

Aryan looked at her. "You came ready to burn it down, didn't you?" he asked.

She gave a faint smirk. "Didn't we always?"

They stepped out of the car and crept toward the back of Unit 6B, hugging the shadows. A dim amber light flickered through frosted glass. There were no guards or cameras. Just silence. Naina whispered, "It's too quiet."

Aryan nodded. "Either they're confident… or already gone."

He tried the door of the side entrance. It was locked.

Naina stepped ahead, pulled a pin from her hair, and began working the old mechanical latch.

Aryan raised an eyebrow. "Seriously?"

She didn't look up. "Do you think I only decode firewalls?"

Click.

The door swung open with a soft creak, and they slipped inside silently. A wave of cold, artificial air greeted them, as did the hum of fans and blinking screens. One of them showed a live satellite feed; another, internal TechNova logs.

Aryan stepped forward and then froze.

A man stood at the far end of the room, his back to them. Crisp dark shirt. Familiar shoulders. Calm.

"Vikram?" Aryan's voice was more a breath than a word.

The figure turned. Vikram Kapoor, TechNova's former Compliance Head, now very much off the grid. His smirk hadn't aged a day.

"Well, well," Vikram said smoothly. "If it isn't Aryan Mehra and Naina Rao. Quite the couple."

Naina instinctively stepped in front of Aryan, "Don't flatter yourself. You're trespassing."

Vikram chuckled. "Oh, I'm not trespassing. *You're* the ones breaking into a secure data relay point. That's what this place is now: a ghost node. Off-book. Invisible."

Aryan's fists clenched. "You sabotaged Mediscan," he accused. "You rerouted funding."

"And yet you have no proof," Vikram said, gesturing to the flickering screens. "Everything wipes clean in two minutes. You're standing inside a dead man's vault."

Naina scanned the setup. "There's a remote kill switch. He's stalling."

Aryan took a step forward. "Why?"

Vikram's smile thinned. "Because truth, Aryan, is only power when people believe it. And people," he looked at Naina, "believe stories, not facts."

A loud *ping* sounded. The screens flickered.

Naina yanked Aryan back. "He activated it. We need to go. Now!"

As they rushed toward the exit, Vikram didn't follow. He stood calmly in the dark, his silhouette framed by falling code.

"Tell Kabir I said hello," he called after them.

Outside, Aryan and Naina didn't stop running until they reached the car, breathless and rattled.

Aryan's fists pounded once against the car roof, a silent scream swallowed by the night.

"We almost had him," he fumed.

"No," Naina said. "Now we know where to look."

Aryan started the car and said, "We're going to Kabir."

***

Chapter 5

THE HIDDEN WAR

They didn't stop driving until they reached the city's central grid. Kabir had responded instantly to Aryan's message, his voice clipped, serious: "Don't come here. Meet Sohail. He's already watching the financial trails."

Now, seated at Café Noir, Aryan and Naina waited for a stranger who allegedly knew more about TechNova's buried secrets than Kabir himself.

The clinking of coffee cups and low jazz couldn't mask the tension at Table 7.

Naina stirred her black coffee without drinking. Aryan sat across from her, eyes scanning the entrance every few seconds.

"Are you sure this place is secure?" she asked, without looking up from her coffee.

"It's neutral, no TechNova eyes, no surveillance," Aryan replied. "Sohail insisted on it."

Naina's brow lifted. "So you trust him more than me now?"

"I didn't say that."

"You didn't have to."

Aryan leaned forward. "Naina, I brought you here because there's something happening inside TechNova, something I can't fix alone."

"You mean beyond the conspiracy, the media trials, and the digital theft?"

He sighed. "Embezzlement. Systemic. Traced to someone with root access. It's not just files anymore, it's money. Lots of it."

Her eyes narrowed. "And you think it's internal?"

"I know it is. And whoever's doing it is making it look like I'm part of it."

Naina finally looked him in the eye. "That's the part that scares you, isn't it? That they're using your systems to dismantle you from inside."

He nodded. "I spent a decade building TechNova," he said quietly. "And now it feels like the walls are folding in."

Before she could respond, a shadow fell across the table.

A man in a grey hoodie and wire-rimmed glasses slid into the third seat.

"You must be Naina," he said, voice low but clear. "I've heard a lot about you."

Naina didn't smile. "That makes one of us."

Sohail leaned back in his chair, unzipping his hoodie halfway to reveal a TechNova visitor badge still clipped to his T-shirt.

Naina's eyes flicked to it, then to Aryan. "You didn't mention he was that close."

Aryan replied, "He's off-books. He does digital security audits on covert contracts. Kabir trusts him."

Naina didn't look convinced. "Being trusted by Kabir is like being trusted by a magician. Impressive, but I still want to see the trick."

Sohail smirked. "I get it. You don't like new people. But I'm not here to be liked; I'm here because I found something that could bury TechNova."

He placed a small drive on the table and slid it toward Aryan.

Naina stopped it with her finger. "No offence, Sohail, but data like this doesn't belong in coffee shops."

"I agree," he said. "But Aryan wanted neutral ground. After what we're about to show you, I doubt we'll be able to meet anywhere public again."

Aryan said nothing. He looked tense, not afraid, but wary.

Naina finally picked up the drive. "What's on it?"

"Bank records, internal fund transfers, phantom vendors, and a trail that leads from TechNova's community outreach budget to offshore accounts."

Aryan leaned in. "How recent?"

"As of last week," Sohail replied. "Someone's still moving money. And they're doing it like they've done it before."

Naina stared at the drive, then back at Sohail.

"Alright," she said. "Let's take this somewhere we can't be overheard."

***

They relocated to Sohail's safehouse, an unmarked flat above a shuttered co-working space. Inside, the windows were blacked out, and the only light came from a cluster of glowing monitors.

Naina stepped in and immediately scanned the room. "Do you run this solo?"

Sohail shrugged. "Trust is expensive. Solitude is cheaper."

Aryan remained near the door, arms crossed, watching as Naina plugged the flash drive into one of Sohail's terminals.

"Are you sure it's clean?" she asked.

"Triple-scrubbed and sandboxed," Sohail replied. "I don't bring malware to a meet-and-greet."

The screen lit up with a string of accounts, each listed under the names of different shell companies.

Naina's brow furrowed. "These aren't just ghost vendors. They're routed through holding firms in Belize, the Caymans, and even Mauritius."

Aryan leaned in. "Where's the source?"

Sohail pulled up the trail. "It starts from TechNova's CSR wing, supposedly donations and community grants. But a huge chunk vanishes before it hits the books."

Naina clicked open a record. "These transfer batches were split over six months," she said. "They are small enough to avoid internal red flags."

Aryan frowned. "That means it was someone who understood our system inside out."

Naina looked at him. "This isn't just internal embezzlement, Aryan. This is a laundering pipeline."

Sohail added, "And whoever's behind it is still active. There's another transfer scheduled in 48 hours."

Aryan said bitterly, "They're stealing from our outreach—from people who needed that help."

"And framing you while they do it," said Naina, her voice cold.

Aryan stared at the monitor, his face a mix of disbelief and dread. The numbers didn't lie, but they felt like a betrayal written in code.

"These are internal fund splits," he murmured. "They have been initiated by someone with finance-level clearance."

Naina folded her arms. "It's someone close to you."

Aryan didn't speak.

"These aren't your average data breaches," Sohail observed. "This is surgical theft, designed to keep you in the dark and take you down with it."

Aryan's voice was low. "How did I not see this?"

Naina didn't answer immediately. Then she said gently, "Because you were fighting fires at the front door, and this came through the basement."

He rubbed his forehead. "I kept pushing transparency protocols. I thought we were too structured for this."

Sohail said, "That's exactly what made it easy. The structure became the blind spot."

Aryan's tone hardened. "Whoever's doing this knows how I think. They built this pipeline inside my rhythm."

Naina walked to the board and wrote down a list of code-named companies. "Then we change the rhythm," she said. "We get ahead."

He looked at her. "Are you still in?"

She met his eyes. "I never left," she said quietly. "I just stopped waiting to be invited back."

Something in Aryan's shoulders relaxed, barely.

Sohail added, "You'll both need to be faster. The next drop hits in under two days."

Naina's voice was firm. "Then we start now. Show me everything."

Lines of code blurred across the screen as Naina navigated through layered databases, bouncing through virtual private networks and firewalls.

Aryan watched her hands fly across the keyboard. "How do you even know where to start?" he asked.

She didn't look up. "You follow the small errors," she replied. "That's where arrogance leaks."

Sohail added, "She's right. Most people cover their footprints, but not their patterns."

Naina paused on a screen with an account disguised under a paediatric charity name.

"This one," she said. "Look at the transfers. They are timed two minutes apart, just under the audit threshold. They're mimicking real-time grant processing."

Aryan leaned closer. "This isn't just one operator; it's a system. A whole architecture."

She opened a connection chart of webs of companies stretching across continents.

"There's a node in Singapore and another in Zurich. This isn't just laundering, it's international laundering," Naina said.

Sohail clicked on a flagged entry. "And this one was routed through a defence supplier in Mumbai."

Aryan froze. "Wait, TechNova was bidding on a medical procurement tender with that same group."

Naina glanced at him. "Then someone's using your reputation to legitimize stolen funds."

Aryan exhaled slowly, his expression darkening. "They're hijacking everything: my name, my company, my work."

Naina looked at him. "Then take it back," she commanded.

There was a long silence before Aryan finally nodded.

"We'll burn it down if we have to," he said. "But we stop this."

Sohail raised an eyebrow. "You're sounding like her now."

Aryan smirked. "That's not a bad thing to sound like."

***

Sohail led them through an alleyway behind the co-working hub and down a narrow stairwell. At the end was a steel door secured with a biometric pad.

"You keep secrets like a spy," Aryan muttered.

"Corporate security is a myth," Sohail replied. "This is control."

The door opened silently, revealing a dim, cool room filled with humming servers and split-monitor stations. Surveillance feeds showed live network activity, power grid fluctuations, and a private dark web feed.

Aryan blinked. "Do you run all this?"

Sohail nodded. "I built it after I left my last contract. Nobody owns me now."

Naina walked straight to the central desk and pulled up a chair. "Good. I need to run a trace on a dummy NGO registered under the name 'Lotus Development Trust'."

Sohail raised an eyebrow in curiosity. "That's part of the CSR laundering scheme?" he asked.

"It's more than that," she said. "I think it's the nerve centre."

Aryan hovered, unsure. "Do you really trust this setup?"

Naina didn't glance back. "I trust what it gives us: time."

Sohail began pulling logs while Naina synced up Kabir's earlier files. "Give me ten minutes and I'll have it mapped against the banking layer," she said.

Aryan sat down, watching the two move with near-telepathic rhythm.

He cleared his throat and remarked, "I've never felt more useful and more useless at the same time."

Naina smirked. "Then stay out of the way, and be quiet. That's useful, too."

Sohail chuckled. "She's missed you."

Aryan didn't respond, but he smiled. The screen flickered and then flashed red:

"UNAUTHORIZED TRACE DETECTED."

Naina's fingers froze mid-keystroke.

"Someone's watching the Lotus node," she said. "We have triggered a silent alarm."

Sohail's tone sharpened. "The firewall's closing. If we don't extract now, we lose the route, and they'll know we were here."

Aryan stood up agitatedly. "What do we do?"

Naina was already typing. "Shut up, and don't breathe."

She launched a mirrored IP cloaking script, fingers dancing like a pianist under pressure. Screens split, duplicated, and bounced signals through three fake endpoints.

Sohail stared. "You're spoofing the spoof?"

She didn't answer. Her eyes were fixed, breath shallow.

A second alert popped up:

"INTRUSION COUNTERMEASURE ENGAGED."

Aryan cursed under his breath. "We're going to get flagged."

"No," Naina muttered. "We're going to win."

Her left hand keyed in a manual portswitch. "Sohail, patch through Frankfurt. Reroute DNS. Now."

He obeyed without question.

Another beat. Then the red screen vanished.

A green confirmation bloomed:

"Access Cloaked. Uplink Secured."

Silence.

Then Sohail whistled. "That... was hot."

Aryan exhaled. "Remind me never to piss you off," he said.

Naina finally leaned back in her chair. "The firewall's down. We're inside the Lotus backbone, everything from vendor logs to personnel entries."

Aryan looked at her, a mix of awe and something softer.

"You never stop surprising me," he said.

Naina raised an eyebrow. "You just stopped paying attention."

Their eyes held for a second longer than necessary.

Then Sohail coughed. "Okay, lovers, back to work."

Aryan cleared his throat. "Right. Show me what these people are hiding."

***

The monitors glowed behind them, quietly pulling data like a living organism. For the first time in hours, the room was still.

Aryan leaned against the table, arms crossed. "Do you ever wonder if we're too late?"

Naina looked up from her screen. "Too late for what?"

"To fix it. The company. Us."

She paused, the cursor blinking on her screen. "It depends on what you're trying to fix."

Aryan exhaled. "I built something I thought was clean. It was disruptive, yes, but ethical. Now it feels like I just gave smarter thieves better tools."

Naina closed her laptop. "You gave people hope," she said gently. "It's not your fault they used it wrong."

"But I let them in," he said. "That part's on me."

After a pause, Naina said quietly, "You were always the architect. But you didn't like patrolling the walls. That's what made you vulnerable."

Aryan's voice cracked a little. "And what made you leave?"

She met his eyes. "That I couldn't watch it crumble from inside. I needed distance to survive it."

A long pause stretched between them.

"You know," he said, "I didn't just call you back for your brain."

She smirked. "You called me because no one else would say it to your face."

He smiled. "And because I missed the only person who never looked at me like a CEO," he said.

Her voice softened. "Don't start getting sentimental."

He didn't answer, but the silence was loaded. Sohail called out from the far terminal, "You two might want to get over here."

Naina walked over quickly, Aryan just behind her.

The screen showed a cluster map of financial movements, glowing in pulses of red and yellow. At the centre, one name pulsed brighter than the rest.

Lotus Foundation.

Aryan's eyes narrowed. "That's our charity partner," he said.

"Yes," Sohail said. "And the digital heart of this entire operation."

Naina scanned the flow paths. “They’re not just laundering money; they’re managing logistics, shipping medical units, funding ghost clinics, creating a paper trail for legitimacy.”

Aryan stepped closer. “We vetted them extensively. Their board’s clean.”

Sohail shook his head. “Only the names you were allowed to see. Dig deeper.”

Naina opened another layer of obscured trustees, hidden donor IDs, and off-ledger procurement. “This isn’t just a front. It’s a shadow company wearing a halo,” she remarked.

Aryan paled. “We launched projects with them—community drives, mobile diagnostics…”

“And they used your brand to build cover,” Naina said, her voice tight. “Every donation from TechNova legitimized their operations.”

Aryan sat down slowly. “No wonder they needed me out of the way. If this went public…”

“...your reputation would take them down with it,” Sohail finished.

The room was silent for a long time.

Then Aryan looked up. “We expose them,” he said. “All of them.”

Naina nodded. “But carefully. We’re not just unmasking fraud; we’re poking a sleeping beast.”

Sohail added, “And beasts bite back.”

Naina paced the length of the room, a clear indication that she was rattled.

“This isn’t a hack-and-leak job,” she said. “This is infiltration. We go into Lotus, we go in deep, and we don’t miss.”

Aryan stood by the server display, arms folded. “What’s our access point?”

Sohail spun around in his chair. “They use a private cloud loop for internal audit. That loop syncs with a secondary server hosted in Dubai.”

“Is it encrypted?” Aryan asked.

“Very securely,” Sohail replied. “But I’ve cracked worse.”

Naina pulled her hair quickly into a knot. “We need to clone their permission layer first,” she said. “Once we enter, the window will close in under ten minutes.”

Aryan looked at both of them. “If we fail, it’s not just a data leak. They’ll know who did it.”

Naina met his gaze. “Then we don’t fail.”

He gave a faint nod. “And if we find what we’re looking for?”

Sohail replied, “Then we burn their temple to the ground.”

Naina began prepping the environment. “I want Kabir on standby,” she said. “If this goes sideways, we’ll need someone to trigger the leak remotely.”

Aryan watched her for a moment. “You plan like someone who’s already seen the worst.”

She glanced over at him. “I have. I just never thought it would wear a foundation’s logo.”

They all turned to the screen as the Lotus login prompt appeared.

Ten minutes. One chance.

***

The Lotus Foundation portal opened with a muted blink. Sohail’s script did its job: masked entry, cloned credentials, and server mirroring.

Naina’s eyes scanned the dashboard. “They’ve buried everything under medical outreach subfolders,” she observed. “Smart.”

Aryan leaned in. “What are we looking at?”

“Clinic reports. Procurement orders. Blood testing campaigns...” Her voice trailed off.

Sohail frowned. “What?”

Naina clicked into one of the folders marked “Phase II: Rural Drive – Bihar”.

What opened wasn’t outreach data. It was profiles, hundreds of them, including names, biometric scans, medical histories, blood types, and organ compatibility data. Aryan’s face paled. “This isn’t just diagnostics.”

“They’re indexing people,” Naina said in a tense voice. “They’re tracking villages with high match ratios.”

Sohail said, “This isn’t CSR; this is human cataloguing.”

Aryan stared, frozen. “You’re saying they’re trafficking?”

Naina didn’t answer, but clicked deeper.

A secondary log showed logistical records, night-time transport, undocumented transfers, and offshore shipping manifests.

“There are no trails, no permissions, all routed through dummy hospitals,” she confirmed.

Aryan said morosely, “We helped fund this.”

His voice broke. Naina reached out but stopped short. Sohail spoke in a low voice, his jaw tight. “We’re not just blowing the whistle now; we’re exposing a global syndicate.”

Aryan said slowly. “If we leak this, they’ll come after us.”

Naina said, “They already are after us, but now we hit back with something that can’t be buried.”

And for the first time, they all looked scared, not for themselves, but for what they’d just uncovered. No one spoke for a long time. The glow from the monitors painted their faces in shades of grim resolve. Naina’s fingers hovered over the keyboard, unmoving. Sohail broke the silence. “This isn’t just about money anymore. This is blood. Flesh. Families.”

Aryan sat down slowly. “We thought we were fighting corruption. Instead, we’re staring at organized exploitation,” he said in a low voice.

Naina finally turned from the screen. “Then the rules have changed, no more restraint.”

Sohail nodded. “If we leak this, they won’t sue. They’ll come hunting.”

Aryan met their eyes. “Then let them. I’d rather go down fighting for truth than stay silent and complicit.”

He looked at Naina. “Are you sure you want to stay in this?”

“I was already in,” she said without hesitation. “Now I’m angry.”

Sohail smirked. “That’s the spirit!”

Naina turned to Aryan. “You’re the face of this company. The moment this data hits daylight, they’ll try to crucify you,” she said.

Aryan shrugged. “Then I stop being the face and start being the fire.”

She smiled, just faintly. "It took you long enough."

Aryan stood up. "So, do we go public?"

"Not yet," said Sohail. "We set the trap first and gather proof that no one can ignore: a full package."

Naina cracked her knuckles. "And then we release it with precision."

Aryan nodded and said, "No drama, just truth, unfiltered and sharp."

They all leaned forward again, their fatigue forgotten.

Now it wasn't about survival; it was about justice.

***

The silence was broken only by the hum of the server for what seemed like ages.

Aryan stood near the whiteboard, dry erase marker in hand, though he hadn't written anything. Naina was seated behind him, arms resting on her knees, gazing steadily at him.

"You could still walk away," he said without turning. "Kabir could set you up abroad. You could disappear and start afresh."

"I'm not disappearing," she replied. "I disappear, they win."

He looked over his shoulder. "Are you sure it's not pride keeping you here?"

Naina gave a dry smile. "Maybe. Or maybe it's unfinished business."

He walked back toward her. "Between us or them?"

She held his gaze. "Both," she replied.

There was a long pause—no tension, just truth between them.

"You and I started this with ideals and a purpose," Aryan said. "And somewhere, I think I let ambition cloud that."

Naina stood up slowly. "And I let silence become distance. We both ran."

He nodded and said softly, "So let's stop running."

She extended her hand. Aryan took it. Just two hands closing a loop.

Sohail, watching from his desk, clapped slowly. "Touching," he said. "Can we get back to bringing down criminal empires now?"

Naina chuckled. "We're ready."

Aryan added, "This time, we're not alone."

Their fingers parted, but something deeper had locked in.

Not romance. Not nostalgia.

Conviction. A promise to finish what they had started and burn the rot at its root.

***

The monitors dimmed. Sohail had gone downstairs to take a call, leaving the two of them alone for the first time since this mess began.

Naina stood by the window, arms folded, staring out into the Bangalore night. The city glowed in silence, unaware of the war brewing behind dark glass.

Aryan walked up behind her, close but not too close.

"You always did like high places," he said softly.

She didn't turn. "I like perspective, something this world keeps stealing from us."

He nodded. "You saved me tonight."

She glanced at him. "You saved yourself. I just reminded you where the light switch was."

A silence followed, thick with everything they hadn't said.

Then, gently, Aryan asked, "Do you regret coming back?"

Naina finally turned to face him. "I regret leaving."

That stopped him cold.

Her voice softened. "I left because I was angry. But I stayed away because I was afraid."

"Of me?"

"No," she said. "Of what I felt when I was with you."

Aryan didn't move. "And now?"

She stepped forward, close enough to feel his breath. "Now I'm just tired of running from it."

He leaned in, not fast, not hesitant. Just certain.

She didn't pull away.

The kiss was soft, unhurried. No fireworks, just the quiet acknowledgement of two storms finally meeting in stillness.

When they pulled back, neither of them spoke. They didn't need to. For now, they had each other. And that was enough.

***

The early hours of the morning bathed the safehouse in cold light. Naina sat at the terminal, eyes half-closed, sifting through log files on autopilot. Aryan was curled up on the couch, not quite asleep, not quite awake.

Sohail returned with two paper cups of *chai*.

"Fuel," he said, handing one to Naina. "And bad news."

She accepted the cup. "What is it now?"

He tapped a folder on the desk. "I got a ping from an old contact in Dubai. The word is that the Lotus Foundation has gone dark; servers shut down, accounts frozen. Someone pulled the plug last night."

Aryan sat up. "Damage control?"

"Or anticipation," Sohail said. "They know we're close. Maybe too close."

Naina's jaw tightened. "So, we scared them."

Sohail shook his head. "No. We *alerted* them."

Aryan stood up, squaring his shoulders. "Then we move faster. What we have isn't enough for the court, but it's enough for the public."

Naina nodded slowly. "I agree. We prepare the release files, evidence, and background context. Everything."

"Once this goes live, there's no pulling back. You'll be targets," Sohail warned.

Aryan looked at both of them. "Then we hit them before they hit us."

There was a long pause.

Then Naina reached for Aryan's hand under the desk.

He didn't flinch.

The war wasn't over; it hadn't even truly begun.

But now they were ready. Together.

And when the storm came, they'd face it with their eyes open.

***

Chapter 6

THE FIRST FRACTURE

The cacophony of the Bangalore market was overwhelming, with vendors shouting, scooters inching between waves of humans. The air smelled of roasting peanuts, incense, and monsoon-soaked asphalt.

Aryan's shirt stuck to his back as he scanned the crowd.

"Any sign of her?" Naina's voice crackled in his earpiece, her tone sharp.

Aryan murmured, "Negative. But she's here. She has to be."

From across the marketplace, Naina moved like she belonged there, unflinching, graceful. Aryan watched her slip between stalls like water through cracks in a stone.

He spotted her pausing near a flower cart.

"Wait," she whispered. "Two o'clock. Behind the textile stand. Green shawl. Clutching something."

Aryan turned. A young woman, eyes wide and restless, stood half-concealed behind a stack of bright saris. Her grip on a thick folder was tight, her knuckles pale.

"That's her," Aryan confirmed. "Don't crowd her. Let me approach her."

He adjusted his pace, weaving past stalls of cardamom, turmeric, and imitation gold. As he neared, the woman's eyes locked with his, uncertain but hopeful.

"Priya Sengupta?" he asked gently.

She gave a jerky nod.

"You're safe," Aryan said. "We're here to listen."

Naina appeared beside him, scanning the surroundings. "Let's walk. Five minutes. Just you, us, and what you've brought."

Priya hesitated, clutching the folder tighter. "I shouldn't be here," she whispered.

Aryan's voice was calm but firm. "Neither should we. But here we are."

Priya took a shaky breath and stepped forward.

***

They ducked into a narrow alley behind the marketplace, quiet, shaded, and just loud enough with ambient city noise to mask a conversation.

Priya's eyes darted left and right. She clutched the folder like it was life itself.

"Take a deep breath," Aryan said gently. "We're not here to hurt you."

"I shouldn't have come," Priya whispered, fingers trembling. "If they find out…"

"They won't," Naina said, cutting in. Her tone was firm, controlled. "Who exactly are you afraid of?"

Priya hesitated.

Naina stepped closer. "Vikram Sharma?"

Priya's breath hitched.

Aryan watched her carefully. "You worked under his unit during the rural health expansion, didn't you?"

Priya nodded slowly.

"What's in the folder?" Naina asked.

"Proof," Priya replied. "Not just money trails, but names, places, real patients, and disappeared ones."

She opened the folder. Inside were printed documents, screenshots, photos, medical records with missing discharge notes, and transport slips with no destinations. Some bore TechNova's outreach seal.

Naina's eyes narrowed. "These clinics… they were funded by Lotus Foundation."

Priya said in a low voice, "But they weren't clinics. They were filters, places to identify viable 'donors'—poor, desperate people who didn't know they were targets."

Aryan looked stunned. "They were harvesting…"

"Yes," Priya said, clutching the folder again. "And I think Vikram is still doing it."

Naina met Aryan's eyes. "We need to move. Fast."

Aryan nodded. "Let's get her somewhere safe. Then we take this apart, page by page."

The apartment wasn't much, with bare walls, a slow ceiling fan, and a kettle that hissed loudly. But it was quiet, and it was safe.

Priya sat at the small dining table, the folder spread open in front of her. Naina leaned over her shoulder, flipping through the contents with surgical precision.

"These aren't just health records," Naina muttered. "They're tagged with numeric codes and bloodwork identifiers."

Aryan stood by the window, phone in hand. "Kabir's on standby. He can verify the hospital logs digitally."

Priya spoke up. "Vikram started hiding the transfers during the mobile diagnostic phase. He said we were streamlining outreach. But files kept vanishing. Patients were never discharged or they were, but with no destination."

Naina paused on a grainy photograph of a woman on a stretcher, her face half-visible. "Did you know her?"

Priya swallowed. "She was pregnant. She came in for anaemia treatment but never left."

Aryan clenched his jaw. "And the board never noticed?"

"They didn't want to," Priya said quietly. "Or they were paid not to."

Naina looked up. "There's a pattern here, a method. This wasn't sloppiness; it was logistics."

Aryan walked to the table. "We need names and access credentials, anything to trace back to Vikram's command trail."

Priya slid a folded slip across the table. "There's one place they never shut down. It's a storage hub and is still active."

Naina met Aryan's eyes. "Then that's where we go next."

***

Naina stared at the address Priya had written. "Basavanagudi? That's not far, but it's too central for a warehouse."

"It's registered as a storage facility under a private logistics group," Priya said. "But no one ever comes in or out during the day. I tracked one late-night shipment, unmarked, no licence plate."

Aryan frowned. "That screams underground."

"And yet, no enforcement agency has touched it," Naina added. "That either means it's protected… or invisible."

Aryan tapped the table lightly. "We need to see it. But not tonight. It's too exposed."

Naina nodded. "We stake it out tomorrow night with a minimal team—just us and Kabir on digital backup."

Aryan glanced at Priya. "You'll stay here. Don't open the door. Don't answer unknown numbers."

"I can't just hide," she said, voice trembling.

"You can," Naina replied, her tone steel-edged. "Because what you gave us could save lives. And if anything happens to you, the rest of the world might never see it."

Priya nodded slowly.

Aryan looked at Naina. "We need burner phones," he said. "Clean wheels. Nothing that ties back to TechNova."

"I'll call Sohail," she said. "He owes me favours."

Aryan raised an eyebrow. "You and Sohail?"

She smirked. "Not like that."

He smiled. "Just checking."

For a moment, the tension cracked briefly. But beneath it was a steady trust. And something else still forming.

"Tomorrow," Aryan said, standing up, "we pull the mask off."

Night pressed in softly around the apartment. The city outside was still buzzing, but inside, things had gone quiet.

Aryan sat on the balcony ledge, staring down at the orange-tinted street. Somewhere below, a hawker's cart clanged as it packed up, ending another city day.

In his lap, his phone showed a live ping from Kabir: "*Tracker ready. Waiting for green light.*"

Behind him, Naina moved silently through the living room, laying out a burner phone, two encrypted drives, and a printed satellite map.

"I forgot how calm you get before things explode," Aryan said.

She didn't look up but retorted, "You get dramatic when you're nervous."

He chuckled. "True."

She joined him on the balcony, folding her arms. The night wind lifted strands of her hair, and for a moment, neither of them spoke.

"Are you okay?" she asked, not softly, but sincerely.

Aryan glanced at her. "You mean aside from the fact that my life's work is now a front for organ trafficking?"

Naina looked away, guilt flickering across her face.

He added gently, "You didn't cause it; you just saw it first."

She hesitated, then said, "I left because I was scared what staying would make me. Now I'm scared of what leaving will cost."

Aryan didn't speak, but he reached over, gently covering her hand on the railing.

She didn't pull away.

The silence settled again, but this time, it felt like an agreement. A pause between two sides of something that was still forming.

Then the phone buzzed again.

"It's time to move," Aryan said.

***

The car rolled down a quiet road in Basavanagudi, headlights dimmed, windows halfway down. Aryan drove while Naina scrolled through a digital map on the burner phone, tracking the coordinates Priya had circled.

"It's that building," she said, pointing ahead. "Grey shutters, no signage. At the corner of the block."

Aryan parked two alleys down and turned off the engine. The building looked desolate. "There's not a soul around," he said. "Not even a guard."

Naina took out a small lens monocular from the glovebox. "Third window from the left, flickering light. Backup servers, maybe."

Aryan glanced at her. "Do you always bring toys?"

"Only when I'm expecting trouble."

She handed him an earpiece and said, "Kabir's patching in now."

There was static. Then Kabir's voice came through:

"You've got signal. That block has heat signatures—two on the ground floor and one upstairs. No external cameras detected."

"Copy that," said Aryan.

Naina pulled her hood up. "We do reconnaissance first—no entry, just eyes."

Aryan looked at her. "I know this drill."

"I'm reminding myself," she said with a slight smile.

They stepped out, shoes soft on the gravel. The warehouse loomed ahead like a forgotten ruin, except they both knew it wasn't.

Aryan whispered, "Whatever's in there, it's still breathing."

Naina replied, "Then we don't let it live much longer."

The warehouse was half-hidden behind a crumbling brick wall overgrown with vines. Aryan crouched low, flashlight off, letting the ambient glow from a streetlamp sketch the outline of the building.

"Back entrance is rusted shut," he whispered into his microphone. "No padlock, but hasn't been opened in weeks."

Naina's voice crackled softly in return. "North side, metal panel door. Reinforced. No handle on the outside."

She emerged from behind a stack of crates at the far side of the alley. Her eyes were sharp, her movements fluid. Aryan met her near the rear loading dock.

"I don't like this," she said. "It's too quiet."

Aryan nodded. "Kabir, heat signatures still holding?"

"Negative," came the voice in their ears. "One just moved. Upstairs, East Quadrant."

Naina's hand immediately slid to the small utility knife at her hip.

Aryan raised an eyebrow. "Knife?"

She whispered back, "Compact, fast, doesn't jam."

A faint creak echoed from inside like a chair dragged across concrete.

They froze.

Then a shadow passed behind one of the upper windows. Slow. Deliberate.

Aryan whispered, "Whoever that is, they're not surprised. They're watching."

Naina's jaw tightened. "Then let's give them something to watch."

She turned, signalling toward a side wall. "We split," she said. "If they want to play, we don't give them one target."

Aryan hesitated for half a second. "Be careful."

"You too," she replied.

Then they disappeared into the dark on opposite flanks, two ghosts hunting a secret.

***

Naina pressed her back against the cold wall, counting her steps as she moved along the side. A service pipe led up toward a half-open ventilation hatch. She paused, crouched, then climbed silently.

Peeking through the slats, she could see into the upper floor: rows of metal cabinets, tagged boxes, and a humming server rack pulsing in blue.

And then, there was a sudden movement.

A man in a grey shirt crossed the room, his face blurred in shadow. He carried a long, heavy case and set it beside a metallic table. He looked calm. Too calm.

Naina whispered into her microphone, "One person confirmed. Upper East Quadrant. Handling cargo."

No reply.

"Copy that?" she asked.

Still nothing.

She cursed under her breath and backed down the pipe, slipping into the alley.

Meanwhile, Aryan circled toward the west side, where the outer fencing gave way to a broken section. As he stepped through, his foot hit something soft, wrapped in cloth.

He knelt to check what he had stumbled against.

It was a bundle. He unwrapped it just enough to see a bloodied lab coat, with the TechNova logo faintly visible on the chest. His breath caught. He reached for his earpiece. "Naina," he said in an urgent whisper. "We've got something. Someone was here. One of ours."

Static.

He tried again. Nothing.

Then he heard footsteps from the shadows behind him, slow and heavy. Aryan stood up, scanning the dark.

"Naina," he said into the microphone, louder now, "we're not alone."

Aryan backed toward the wall, the footsteps drawing closer to him. He kept his stance loose, palms steady. His earpiece hissed, still no signal.

From the corner, a figure emerged.

It was not Vikram, but not random either.

Black cargo pants. Gloves. An earpiece.

Aryan raised his voice just enough and asked, "Security? Or hired muscle?"

The man didn't answer. Instead, he advanced, swiftly and confidently.

Aryan didn't wait. He turned and ran, weaving through the fencing, knocking over a loose bin to buy a few seconds.

Naina had already circled back and was crouched near the entry ramp. She spotted Aryan and instantly realized what was happening.

"Run?" she asked.

"Run," he replied, panting.

Behind them, two more shadows appeared. No sirens. No voices. Just pursuit.

They darted into the maze of alleyways behind the warehouse. Aryan turned a sharp left, vaulting over a pile of stacked crates. Naina followed him.

"We need an exit route," she hissed into the microphone.

Finally, Kabir's voice came through faintly:

"You've got a parallel lane two blocks east. Leads to the main road. I've got a bike waiting."

Naina didn't question him. "Let's move," she said, grabbing Aryan's wrist. As they turned the last corner, Aryan tossed something into the dark behind them, a small tracker with a blinking red light.

"Let them chase us," he said. "We've already marked the place."

They vanished into the shadows.

And for the first time, the hunters were leaving breadcrumbs of their own.

***

The safehouse was a borrowed studio flat above a shuttered café. Kabir had secured it two hours before the operation. One mattress. One table. One hanging bulb. It was enough.

Aryan pulled off his jacket. "They weren't amateurs," he said, still catching his breath.

Naina dropped her bag and immediately laid out the bloodied lab coat. "This changes everything. Someone from inside TechNova was there recently."

Kabir, perched by the only window with a laptop, nodded. "That coat was tagged in our inventory system. It was donated to the Lotus field unit six weeks ago."

Aryan ran a hand through his hair. "We thought we were chasing paperwork," he said. "This is personnel."

Naina flipped the coat inside out. There, in tiny inked numbers near the seam - "SR-4".

She looked up. "That's not a unit number. That's a subject code."

Kabir's fingers clacked on the keyboard. "Confirmed. 'SR' tags were used in one of Vikram's pilot programmes for biometric matching. But those files were buried deep."

Aryan stared at the blinking screen. "So Vikram never shut the system down; he just moved it."

Kabir added, "And whatever's still running is mobile, protected, and connected to people who don't hesitate to send muscle."

Naina crossed her arms. "We need to rethink the timeline," she said, frowning. "This isn't a legacy scandal. It's happening now."

Aryan met her eyes. "Then let's stop thinking like investigators."

She arched a brow. "You're suggesting…?"

"We start thinking like saboteurs."

***

Kabir angled his laptop toward them. "If we hit their communications node, we can expose the relay they're using to move data off-grid."

Naina leaned in. "You mean breach from inside the shell company?"

"Exactly. Arkaris Holdings is still registered under Vikram's old contact, but now it's masking a real-time sync system buried in Lotus's backend."

Aryan paced the room. "Can we trigger a delay loop? Something that buys us time while we extract?"

Kabir grinned. "You really have been listening."

"Only when you stop being annoying," Aryan shot back.

Naina interrupted, her tone sharp. "Focus. We don't just need the data; we need to redirect it. We need to leak it, but only after we have full chains of proof, no partial drops."

Kabir typed fast. "Then we mirror their server behaviour, inject trackers, trigger backups, and plant a signature that points back to Vikram."

Aryan crossed his arms. "False breadcrumbs?"

"Real ones," Kabir replied. "Just delivered on our terms."

Naina nodded. "We'll need a field diversion, too," she said. "Something to draw them out during the upload. They'll have fail-safes, probably off-site response teams."

Aryan looked at her. "How loud are we ready to go?"

She hesitated. "Loud enough to wake the city, but quiet enough not to get arrested."

Kabir cracked his knuckles. "Give me eight hours. Then we ghost their system from the inside out."

Aryan smiled. "Now we're fighting back."

***

There was silence in the room.

Kabir had gone out for food and burner SIMs.

Naina sat cross-legged on the floor, scrolling through surveillance stills. Aryan sat across from her, elbows resting on his knees, watching her more than the screen.

"Do you ever think about what life was supposed to look like by now?" he asked, voice low.

She didn't glance up. "All the time. Then I open folders like Priya's and remind myself why it doesn't."

He smiled faintly. "You're still angry."

She finally looked at him. "Aren't you?" she asked.

Aryan nodded. "Yes, but not just at them. I'm angry at myself, too, for not seeing it, and for letting it happen under my name."

Naina studied him. "You didn't cause it," she said gently. "But you can end it."

Their eyes held for a moment too long.

"You scare me, you know," he said.

Her brows lifted. "I scare you?"

"You walk into fire like it owes you answers."

She smirked. "And you still follow."

"I always have."

The silence that followed wasn't awkward. It was heavy, thick with meaning, with timing, with all the things they hadn't said since she came back.

Then her voice softened. "When this is over…"

Aryan's gaze didn't waver. "It's not over yet," he said expressionlessly.

But his hand reached out, slowly, deliberately, and found hers resting on the floor.

She didn't pull away.

***

It was midnight.

The safehouse lights were off. From the window slit, only the faintest hum of Outer Ring Road could be heard. Kabir's screen cast a cold glow across the room.

"We're in," he said. "Mirror relay activated. Their data hub is syncing live with ours now. I give us twelve minutes before they notice."

Aryan and Naina looked over his shoulder, eyes locked on the scrolling lines of code.

"What are we pulling?" Aryan asked.

"Everything," Kabir replied. "Transaction chains, biometric tags, patient logs, and even shadow payroll. They kept no firewall between the criminal and the corporate."

Naina leaned in. "Inject the beacon now. Tie the files to Vikram's login path."

"Already done," Kabir said. "But there's something else."

He tapped into a folder buried three levels deeper than the others. It opened slowly, heavily encrypted.

Inside were video files.

Aryan frowned. "What is this?"

Kabir clicked one.

It showed a dim room. There was a restrained figure on a gurney and medical equipment running. A voice off-screen was asking questions in Hindi. Clinical. Cold.

Aryan's face hardened. "They filmed it."

Naina swallowed. "This is proof. Not just paper but faces. People."

Kabir said nothing. His fingers were flying over the keyboard now.

"I'm splitting the video stream, one copy to the server and one backup to our offline vault," he said.

Aryan said in a low voice, "This changes everything."

Kabir nodded. "Only if we survive the upload."

Suddenly, the console flashed red:

"External access detected."

"They're onto us," said Naina in an expressionless voice.

Aryan reached for his phone. "Then we trigger the final push. Now."

The server blinked red twice:

"Connection override detected. Countermeasure active."

Kabir's voice stayed calm, but his fingers moved fast. "They've initiated a system-wide wipe. If we don't finish the pull now, we lose everything."

Aryan leaned in. "How much longer?"

Kabir muttered, "Sixty seconds. Maybe less."

Naina stood by the door, eyes on the hallway. "Backup location?"

Kabir nodded. "I am transmitting to a cold vault node I built last year, air-gapped, no IP trail."

Aryan's phone buzzed. A single message flashed:

"Leave. You're being watched."

No sender.

He showed it to Naina.

"We're compromised," she said. "This isn't just a remote trace; they're closing in physically."

Kabir swore under his breath. "I'm uploading the final node."

Aryan grabbed the drive Kabir handed him. It was sealed, encrypted, and labelled with only one symbol—the head of Nandi, etched in obsidian.

"You go out the back," Kabir said. "I'll spoof a dummy signal and delay their trace."

Naina's jaw tensed. "We leave together."

"Not this time," Kabir replied, already jamming a signal booster into the wall. "You have the data. That's what matters now."

Aryan looked at him. "Don't do anything heroic."

Kabir cracked a grin. "It's not heroism; it's chess."

Naina squeezed Kabir's shoulder. "Make them chase ghosts."

"We're good at that," he said.

Aryan and Naina slipped out the back exit just as the lights flickered.

Behind them, Kabir disappeared into the screen glow.

Aryan and Naina didn't look back.

They ran, not just to escape, but to finish what they had started.

***

Chapter 7

GHOSTS IN THE SYSTEM

Kabir slid his headphones on and leaned back in his creaky chair, one leg tucked under the other like he was settling in for a late-night jam session. On the screen was a live grid of digital tunnels and encrypted nodes, blinking red like warning flares.

"Alright, Vikram," he muttered. "Let's dance."

Lines of code scrolled across the monitor like a heartbeat gone wild. Kabir cracked his knuckles, fingers twitching with the rhythm only hackers seem to hear.

From the sofa nearby, Sohail raised a brow. "Do you always talk to the firewall before breaking it?"

Kabir grinned. "Only when it deserves foreplay."

He launched the first script, Nandi Echo, a worm built to mimic admin traffic, clean and near invisible. Instantly, the server responded with static walls of firewalled junk data.

"Cute," Kabir said, eyes sparkling. "You made it personal."

Sohail leaned in. "Are we sure we want to do this now? Gala's already underway. Aryan and Naina are in position."

Kabir didn't look away from the screen. "Exactly. While they sip champagne and shake hands, we ghost through the firewall."

He triggered a ghost protocol to cloak his trail through five proxy servers across three continents.

First wall breached.

A small beep. A blinking green dot.

Sohail grinned. "One down?" he asked.

Kabir nodded. "One down. Four to go. And this time, we're not just stealing data."

He clicked into the second node. "We're setting fire to a legacy."

***

The gala was a waltz of wealth, tinkling laughter, crystal chandeliers, and glasses filled with liquids, the names of which no one could pronounce. Aryan adjusted the cuff of his navy blazer as he stepped through the doors, posture loose, smile calculated.

Beside him, Naina looked elegant in a matte black saree with an embroidered border. Her sharp eyes scanned the room, not missing a single face.

"We're officially underdressed," Aryan murmured.

"You're in a tailored suit," she replied.

"Exactly. They'll think I'm trying to prove something."

Naina smirked. "You are."

They moved through the crowd like seasoned diplomats. Aryan nodded at two investors he recognized but didn't approach them. Naina paused near a glass sculpture, pretending to admire it while syncing her watch's pulse monitor with Kabir's uplink.

"Status?" she whispered.

Kabir's voice came softly through the hidden earpiece. "One wall down. Moving to the second. They haven't detected me yet."

Aryan tilted his head subtly. "Do you see him?" he asked.

Naina's gaze swept the ballroom. "Not yet. But if Vikram's here, he won't be hiding. He'll want to be seen."

"Flamboyant. As always," Aryan said. "What's our angle?"

Naina stepped closer. "We don't corner him. We orbit, draw him in."

Aryan smiled. "Seduction through strategy. You've grown sharper."

She met his eyes, steady. "You stopped seeing clearly," she said.

Before he could reply, the crowd parted.

And there he was.

Vikram Sharma.

Dressed in ivory, drink in hand, smile like a blade.

"Game on," Naina said under her breath.

***

Kabir leaned forward, fingers dancing over the keyboard with the urgency of someone defusing a bomb but enjoying it far too much.

The second firewall wasn't just code; it was personality.

Lines of reactive encryption shifted in real-time, adapting to his moves like a digital chess master.

"Ohhh," he breathed, eyes glinting. "You've upgraded, Vikram. I'm flattered."

Sohail hovered nearby, chewing a pen cap. "That adaptive layer wasn't there last time," he said worriedly.

Kabir grinned. "That's because we weren't this close last time."

He launched a scatter protocol with five simultaneous spoof attempts aimed at the node's validation system. One failed, two bounced, and the fourth triggered an internal lockout.

The fifth slipped through. "Boom!" Kabir said triumphantly.

But just as the system allowed access, red lines lit up the screen: "Trace Activated. Reverse Ping Inbound."

Sohail stiffened. "Have they spotted it?"

"Not yet," Kabir said, typing faster. "It's an automated deadman switch. If we're not careful, it'll loop back to our exact IP."

Sohail moved to the router. "Switching circuit paths now."

Kabir worked a second console, rerouting his digital fingerprint through a series of civilian proxies, including a law firm in Geneva and a bakery in Gujarat.

The screen dimmed.

Access held.

"Trace deflected," Kabir said, exhaling. "Firewall Two breached. It was a real bouncer."

Sohail asked, "What now?"

Kabir smiled. "Now we walk into the vault."

***

Aryan sipped his drink without tasting it, nodding at a guest who'd just launched into a story about real estate in Goa. Beside him, Naina laughed politely, but her eyes never stopped moving.

"Third cluster near the bar," she whispered behind the rim of her wine glass. "Those two with the lapel pins. They've done work for Vikram's NGO."

Aryan didn't look directly at them. "Lotus Foundation?"

"They are alumni of their 'medical logistics' initiative, paid through Arkaris Holdings."

Aryan excused himself from the Goan investor with a handshake and stepped with Naina into the quieter side of the ballroom, which had dim lighting and fewer listeners.

Kabir's voice pinged into their earpieces. "Second wall's down. System responded. They know something's moving."

Aryan murmured, "How long until you hit their core node?" His voice stayed casual, but the muscles in his jaw betrayed him.

"Five minutes if they don't kick me out. Ten if they do."

Aryan turned slightly as a server passed. "Do you ever think we're being watched from both sides?"

"All the time," Naina replied. "But it's only a problem if we freeze."

Just then, a woman in a shimmering green gown approached them. "Mr Mehra, Ms Rao, how lovely to see you again," she gushed.

Aryan's smile didn't reach his eyes as he greeted her, "Anita."

"Vikram said you might drop in," she said, her voice dripping civility.

Naina stepped forward. "And what else does Vikram say when we're not around?"

Anita's smile widened. "He says you're always watching. And that makes him… careful."

Aryan replied, "Then he finally learned something."

***

Kabir's fingers froze for just a second. The screen flickered once, then again.

Then the text changed: "WELCOME BACK, KABIR."

Sohail leaned in. "Is that… part of the system?"

Kabir's jaw tightened. "That's not code. That's a message."

The interface pulsed red. Suddenly, data lines twisted, coiling into recursive loops, encryptions folding in on themselves, like a digital Rubik's Cube reconfiguring mid-air.

"Vikram's using an adaptive defence AI," Kabir muttered. "It's not blocking me; it's watching how I play."

Sohail stepped toward the breaker switch. "We pull out?"

Kabir shook his head. "No. This is where the fun begins."

He launched a mirror-dive protocol, sending a false version of himself into the AI's attention funnel, an echo that mimicked every keystroke from ten seconds ago. The system latched on.

And Kabir dropped under its line of sight.

"Got you!" he exclaimed exultantly.

Sohail exhaled. "You're actually enjoying this, aren't you?"

Kabir grinned, sweat beading near his temple. "It thinks I'm trying to breach the finance wing. But we're already in the personnel core."

He opened a concealed sub-folder labelled "FieldOps_Confidential".

Inside were travel logs, coded IDs, real names, and photos.

"Good heavens!" he said. "They're running a real-time dispatch model for medical transports, the kind that never come back."

Sohail frowned. "That's organ movement scheduling."

Kabir's voice dropped. "And some of the drop points match TechNova's own outreach zones."

The AI stirred again, sensing redirection.

Kabir steadied himself. "We're staying in," he said. The back of his neck prickled with the familiar heat of being hunted. "This system's smart, but it's not angry yet."

He typed faster.

"We wait until it panics."

***

Vikram Sharma approached like a man who owned the room, posture regal, suit immaculate, charm turned to just the right temperature.

"Aryan. Naina," he greeted, lifting his glass. "I would say it's a surprise, but you've never been good at staying off the radar."

Aryan's smile was slight. "And you've never been good at staying out of the shadows."

Vikram chuckled. "Touché."

Naina kept her expression neutral, her fingers gently tapping the clutch she carried. "Busy evening. You seem... unbothered."

"Should I be bothered?" Vikram asked, eyes glittering. "It's just a fundraiser. For public health, no less."

"You've always had a soft spot for optics," said Aryan.

Vikram leaned forward. "Optics matter, especially when one's former company is under investigation for internal leaks and reputational decline," he taunted in a low voice.

Naina didn't blink. "And when your name resurfaces in those investigations?"

"It's baseless gossip," Vikram said, sipping his drink. "Besides, no one ever proves anything in this country, not unless they want to disappear."

Aryan's jaw tightened, but he didn't react.

Vikram smiled broadly. "Relax. I'm not here to quarrel. I'm here just to watch the dance and perhaps... remind you that digging too deep sometimes collapses the ground beneath you."

He raised his glass slightly. "Enjoy the wine, but remember, the walls are thinner than you think."

Then he turned and disappeared into the crowd, leaving behind only the taste of polished menace.

Naina whispered, "He knows."

Aryan replied, "Let him. That means he's nervous."

***

Kabir narrowed his eyes as the screen shifted from code to something else entirely—cleaner smoother, almost elegant.

The core wasn't just a server interface. It was a designed experience.

"Okay, that's new," he muttered. "Vikram went premium."

The central node unfolded like a digital sculpture, four glowing spheres, each labelled in code: "INTAKE", "EVALUATION", "TRANSFER", "CLEARANCE".

Sohail stood behind him, silent. "Is this a patient processing system?"

Kabir nodded slowly. "Not for treatment. For trafficking."

He accessed the EVALUATION module.

Inside were layered profile images, biometric scans, blood reports, and even genetic flags. The data was tagged with codenames, timestamps, and priority labels.

"Some of these are current," Kabir said, his voice tight. "As in, active this week."

He flipped to the TRANSFER module.

Inside was a list of names matched to logistics terminals across India, Dubai, and eastern Europe.

Sohail leaned closer. "They're moving people like inventory."

Kabir pulled up the CLEARANCE protocol.

It required a key, not just an encryption key, but a biometric one. Kabir frowned. "The final access point needs a physical scan," he said. "Probably Vikram's."

The interface flickered suddenly. A new message appeared:

"You've come too far, friend."

Sohail muttered, "The system knows we're here."

Kabir didn't move. "We have what we need. But we're not done."

He copied the profiles and the transport logs, then packaged them into a secure burst file.

"Ready for dispatch," he whispered. "Now we wait for Aryan's signal."

The game was no longer about breach. It was about exposure.

***

Vikram stood near the antique fountain, surrounded by a trio of industrialists laughing too hard at nothing. Aryan and Naina approached together, casual but alert.

"You're still the centre of attention," Aryan said, lifting his glass in mock salute.

Vikram turned, smile reloaded. "I can't help it. Old habits die hard."

Naina's voice was pleasant. "We heard Lotus Foundation is planning an expansion into the Northeast. Rural clinics?"

"We're always expanding," Vikram replied smoothly. "Where there's need, we respond."

Aryan sipped his drink. "Be careful," he said. "The more you build, the more paperwork piles up. And sometimes, paper talks."

Vikram chuckled. "Ah, Aryan! Are you still clinging to this righteous whistleblower fantasy?"

"It's not a fantasy," Naina said. "We just prefer transparency, even when it's inconvenient."

Vikram tilted his head. "Do you think you're intimidating me? Please. You're both out of practice and out of allies."

Aryan stepped closer, lowering his voice. "Do you think data can't speak? It can scream, Vikram. And it's beginning to do so."

A flicker passed over Vikram's face, brief but real. Then the mask returned. "Big words," he said. "But talk is cheap. And so is noise." He leaned in just slightly. "But one wrong echo... and sometimes, things break."

Naina smiled. "Only when they're already cracked."

Kabir's voice pinged softly in their earpieces: "All files secured. Waiting on your go."

Aryan gave a subtle nod. "Then let's make some noise," he said.

They clinked glasses with Vikram, each person's smile more artificial than that of the next.

The war had moved into the open.

***

The screen froze, not in a system crash, but as if it were waiting. Kabir frowned. "That's not a glitch. That's a decision point."

Sohail leaned in. "Meaning?"

Kabir pointed to the blinking prompt:

"AUTHENTICATE OR WITHDRAW."

Below it was a question:

"What did you lose to learn loyalty?"

Kabir blinked. "What on earth is this?"

Sohail murmured, "Is it a security question?"

Kabir shook his head. "No," he said decisively. "It's a taunt. Vikram embedded a logic wall, something only I would see."

Sohail tensed. "You think he knew you'd come?"

Kabir's lips thinned. "He always played two games at once."

He stared at the question, his fingers hovering over the keys.

Flashbacks blurred behind his eyes—mentors-turned-liars, whistleblowers erased from records, and Aryan's early days at TechNova, back when they both believed they were building something pure.

He typed: "Silence".

The screen blinked.

Then unlocked.

Kabir exhaled. "He wanted to see if I'd blink."

Sohail looked rattled. "That was... eerie."

Kabir entered the core registry. Final logs appeared, confirming not just organ movement, but financial trails—transfers routed through health contracts, feeding into shell accounts.

He encrypted it into a burst packet and added one more layer, a public fail-safe.

"If we disappear," he said, "this goes live worldwide."

Sohail nodded. "This isn't a breach anymore. This is exposure."

Kabir smiled faintly. "Good. I want him to feel naked."

***

The ballroom pulsed with laughter and champagne. Aryan and Naina slipped out a side corridor that opened onto a dim garden patio lined with manicured hedges and string lights.

They didn't speak at first but just stood there, breathing in the fresh air.

"We have the files," Aryan finally said, his voice low. "Kabir's almost through."

Naina nodded, her eyes on the small fountain bubbling near a stone bench. "We've never been this close to actual justice."

Aryan glanced at her. "And yet you look... restless."

She leaned against the railing. "That's because I know what happens next. Retaliation. Noise. Denial. Damage control."

Aryan stepped beside her. "You've changed."

She turned and said with a faint smile, "So have you."

He studied her closely for a moment.

"You have stopped waiting for permission," he said. "You lead now, even when it hurts."

She looked down. "And you have stopped hiding behind vision speeches. You fight now, without worrying if your hands get dirty."

Their eyes locked. No more smiles. No more sarcasm. Just honesty. Naina spoke first. "Do you ever wonder if we missed our window?"

Aryan shook his head. "I think we just waited for the right war."

After a pause, he stepped closer, slowly, deliberately, until there was nothing between them but history.

She didn't step back. Not this time. He reached up and brushed a strand of hair behind her ear.

And then quietly, with no drama, they kissed.

It wasn't urgent; it was earned.

***

The cursor blinked against a black background. One final keystroke ENTER, and the vault opened.

Kabir didn't flinch. He had expected encrypted folders, maybe high-level internal documents. But what appeared on the screen stunned even him: "GLOBAL NODE: SYNDICATE PIPELINE".

Sohail leaned forward. "That's not TechNova's server anymore, is it?"

Kabir shook his head slowly. "No. This is something else. This is Vikram's actual empire."

A live map unfolded routes stretching from Chennai, Hyderabad, and Lucknow, feeding into ports in Colombo, Istanbul, and Rotterdam.

Each node pulsed with live data—cargo tags, shipping IDs, and patient biometric IDs masked as supply inventory.

"It's not just data laundering," Kabir said, his voice tight. "It's human routing—organ tracking. Real-time."

He clicked open a secondary folder marked “Clearance Contracts”.

Inside were scanned passports, shadow ID cards, medical tags, and payment receipts in multiple currencies: USD, EUR, and AED.

Sohail swallowed. “That’s black-market clearance… for live donors.”

Kabir leaned back, his breath shaky for the first time. For a second, the enormity of it all cracked through his defences. “It’s not a scandal,” he said incredulously. “It’s a marketplace.”

He tapped a final command, encrypting everything into a burst relay tagged for Aryan and Naina.

“This goes to them now. If anything happens here…”

“I know,” Sohail said, already moving toward the emergency cutoff switch.

Kabir nodded. “It’s not just about revenge anymore.”

“It’s exposure,” Sohail finished. “And consequences.”

The final file zipped, encrypted and ready for dispatch.

Kabir said, “Let’s finish this now.”

***

The vibration on Aryan’s watch was subtle but unmistakable.

He pulled back from Naina, the kiss still hovering between them, and glanced at the alert on his screen:

“TRANSFER COMPLETE. CONTENT: PHOENIX VAULT. STATUS: LIVE.”

She leaned in. “Kabir?”

He nodded. “We’ve got it. All of it.”

Her eyes sharpened immediately. “We need to leave. Now.”

He held her gaze and said, “The second we walk back in there, we’re targets.”

“Correction,” Naina said, fixing her hair with calm precision. “We’ve always been targets. Now we’re also dangerous.”

They re-entered the gala, slipping seamlessly into the crowd. Music played. Glasses clinked. But beneath the glitter, the room felt charged.

Across the hall, Vikram stood in quiet conversation with a foreign delegate. His body was still, but his eyes…

They scanned. Hunted.

He knew.

Aryan whispered, "What happens if he makes a move?"

Naina didn't hesitate. "Then we let him. And we record everything."

Aryan checked the file on his secure drive, which was fully synced. "Kabir duplicated the route," he said. "One copy here. One offline. One more ready for public drop if we vanish."

"Fail-safe," she said. "Just like we planned."

They moved closer to the exit, slowly, deliberately, brushing shoulders with allies and enemies alike.

No sudden moves.

Not yet.

Naina leaned close. "The game's not over yet."

Aryan replied, "No. It's finally begun."

***

Aryan adjusted his cufflink as they moved back into the main ballroom, the swell of music and polite conversation enveloping them like a velvet curtain.

Naina was half a step ahead, her posture perfect, her face unreadable. She scanned the room in micro-movements—exit routes, known faces, and subtle shifts in body language.

"Two tails," she murmured. "Security-grade posture. Not gala regulars."

Aryan didn't glance around. "Hired?"

"Loyal, which might be worse."

They passed by a group of board members, clinking glasses. Naina smiled at them. Aryan nodded. Just another power couple enjoying a glamorous night.

Kabir's voice came softly through their earpieces. "I've scrubbed your digital signatures. You're ghosts again. But Vikram's watching. Don't make it obvious."

Aryan exhaled slowly. "We're walking out the front door. Calm. Untouched."

"Elegant," Naina added, the corner of her mouth lifting.

They slowed near the main display, a diamond-studded model of a mobile clinic. Aryan tapped the placard absently, pretending to read.

"Poetic," he muttered. "Trafficking wrapped in philanthropy."

Naina's voice was low. "He always was a showman."

They reached the main foyer. A valet looked up, already extending a hand for Aryan's parking token.

From behind them, a voice called out.

"Aryan."

They turned.

Vikram stood near the archway. Alone. No guards. No glass in hand. Just a smile.

"A pleasure, as always," he said.

Aryan returned the smile. "We'll be in touch."

Naina held Vikram's gaze for one beat longer.

Then they turned and walked out slowly, silently, and victoriously.

For now.

***

The screen showed a single command: "UPLOAD: YES / NO".

Kabir cracked his neck gently and reached for the thermos on the desk. He hadn't touched his coffee. It was cold now, but he drank it anyway.

Sohail stood at the window, peeking past the curtain. "Aryan and Naina just got into the car. We're clear."

Kabir nodded. "Then it's time."

He clicked 'YES'.

The encrypted burst relay was activated, routing the files through multiple dead drops and dormant journalist inboxes. Not immediate. Not reckless. But traceableto the right people.

"Distribution cycle begins in sixty minutes," Kabir said. "Unless I cancel it. Which I won't."

Sohail sat down, staring at the matrix of moving files. "Do you ever wonder what this will actually change?"

Kabir didn't answer immediately. Then he said, "Truth doesn't guarantee change. But it ruins comfort. And that's a start." He encrypted a secondary copy and labelled it with a simple file tag: "ASHES_REMAIN".

"Dramatic," remarked Sohail.

Kabir shrugged. "When you burn a man's lies, you leave him with ashes. Let's make sure he chokes on them."

The final server pulsed once, then went still, digital heartbeat fading into silence. Kabir leaned back, watching the screen.

"Done."

Sohail gave a slow nod. "Then what now?"

Kabir smirked. "Now we wait for the system to scream."

***

The city lights blurred past the car windows as Aryan drove, one hand on the wheel, the other resting loosely in his lap. Naina sat beside him in her gala saree, heels kicked off, her eyes fixed out the window.

Neither of them spoke for a while.

Finally, Aryan broke the silence. "We did it."

Naina turned to him. "We started it."

He nodded slowly. "Kabir?"

She checked her watch. "Files are out. Timer's running. In forty-five minutes, the first leak goes live."

Aryan exhaled. "After that, there's no containing it," he said.

"There's no protecting anyone either," she added. "No shields. No legal buffers."

Aryan's jaw tightened. "Good."

Naina looked at him. "You're not afraid anymore, are you?"

"I'm tired of being afraid," he said. "Of my company. Of my name. Of ghosts with money and surgical gloves."

She studied him, this man who once hid behind keynote speeches and digital dreams.

"You've changed," she said.

"So have you."

Their hands met in the space between them, fingers locking without ceremony.

Outside, the city pulsed on. Unaware. Unready.

But inside the car, a war had already begun.

Aryan looked ahead. “The world’s going to know everything,” he said. And for once, he wasn’t thinking about redemption; he was thinking about reckoning.

Naina squeezed his hand. “And they’ll know who stood up first.”

The skyline of Bangalore glimmered in the distance.

Unforgiving. Alive. Waiting.

***

Chapter 8

ALLIES IN THE ASHES

The road narrowed as they approached the resort, dust curling behind the car, trees pressing in from both sides. Bangalore was far enough behind to feel irrelevant. Ahead, there was only stillness and intent.

Aryan slowed the car as the gates came into view, elegant but discreet. It was the kind of place that hosted off-record meetings, not weddings.

Naina checked her watch. "We're ten minutes early."

Aryan glanced at her. "Are you nervous?"

She gave him a sidelong glance. "I'm not the one who used to argue with Lakshmi Iyer on national panels."

"She liked the sound of her voice too much," Aryan muttered.

"She liked facts," Naina corrected. "You hated being corrected."

He smiled, briefly. "Touché."

They pulled into a stone-paved courtyard. A uniformed attendant opened the gate. No questions asked. Clearly, someone had already cleared their names.

As they stepped out of the car, Aryan looked up at the colonial-style facade. "She picked this place on purpose," he said.

Naina nodded. "Private, neutral, outside surveillance radius."

They walked silently toward the reception hall.

"She'll test us," Aryan warned.

"She'll test you," Naina replied. "I already passed."

He shot her a look, and she smiled at him. But behind the smile, the storm churned quietly. Beneath the humour was focus. And beneath that, tension.

Not with each other.

With the world they were about to step deeper into.

***

The resort's lounge was warm with wood-panelled walls, soft lighting, and silence too intentional to be casual. Aryan and Naina stood near a window, looking at the gardens, as footsteps approached, measured, confident, unfaltering.

"Welcome to the eye of your storm," came a voice from behind.

They turned.

Lakshmi Iyer stood in a crisp cream saree with a slate-grey border. No jewellery except a single silver ring. Her smile was gentle, but far from soft.

"Aryan Mehra," she said. "Still taller than your opinions, I see."

Aryan smirked. "Lakshmi Iyer. Still walking into rooms like you built them."

She extended a hand. "Built a few. Watched others burn."

Naina stepped forward. "Thank you for agreeing to meet us," she said.

Lakshmi turned to her with genuine warmth. "You've grown sharper. And quieter. That makes you dangerous."

Naina smiled. "I've had practice."

They sat at a round table set with a decanter of water and untouched glasses. No staff lingered nearby. Everything about the scene felt curated and intentional.

Lakshmi poured herself a glass of water and took a sip. Then she looked at Aryan. "Let's not pretend this is about catching up," she said. "You're here because you've hit a wall. And you need someone who knows how to walk through them." There was no kindness in her voice, only realism.

Aryan said nothing.

Naina spoke instead. "We have a name. A trail. And a list of enemies we can't fight alone."

Lakshmi's eyes gleamed. "Then you've come to the right enemy of the state."

***

Lakshmi placed a slim folder on the table and tapped it once.

"Vikram Sharma isn't hiding behind corporate lawyers anymore," she said. "He's wrapped in something far more effective than bureaucracy and fear."

Aryan leaned forward. "Meaning?"

She opened the folder. Inside were newspaper clippings, internal memos, and annotated org charts.

"He doesn't operate alone; he never did. He's the bridge between private exploitation and political protection. And that bridge has pillars in assembly, in the police, in the press."

Naina scanned the papers. "This memo is from the Ministry of Health."

Lakshmi nodded. "It's about a policy tweak last year that made it easier for private foundations to 'fast-track' medical procurement. Vikram's NGO got the first exemption."

Aryan's voice hardened. "And no one questioned it?"

"They questioned. They just didn't publish," Lakshmi replied. "Control the editors, and you control the noise."

She flipped the chart to show names connected by red lines, some familiar, others shocking.

"He's been shielded by two MLAs, one retired Home Secretary, and at least one senior officer in Police Services."

Naina looked up. "So we're not just fighting a man, we're fighting a network."

Lakshmi's tone sharpened. "You're fighting a machine. And it doesn't like being exposed."

Aryan's jaw clenched. "What about allies?" he asked. "Is there anyone inside the system who hasn't sold out?"

Lakshmi smiled slightly. "One. Maybe two. But they come with risk."

Naina asked, "Names?"

Lakshmi closed the folder. "Avaneesh Kumar and Rajesh Kumar. One commands men; the other commands silence."

Aryan sat back, his eyes narrowing.

So the war had a new map.

And now, it had names.

Aryan frowned as he stared at the name circled in Lakshmi's folder: Commandant Avaneesh Kumar.

"Paramilitary officers from CRPF who don't usually mix with civilian firestorms," he said. "They have rules. Chains of command. Quiet pensions."

Lakshmi raised an eyebrow. "Avaneesh isn't typical."

Naina leaned forward. "Gallantry medallist. Incorruptible. Unshaken. Posted to some of the toughest operations in the country."

Aryan crossed his arms. "And now he's going to walk into a political swamp just because we ask?"

"He already has," Naina said calmly. "Lakshmi briefed him discreetly last week. He's been tracking similar corruption in procurement channels. He just didn't have names."

Aryan turned to Lakshmi. "And what makes you so sure he's clean?"

She didn't blink. "Because I've watched him bury his own career protecting men who had no one else. And he never cashed in the favours."

"And Rajesh Kumar?" Aryan asked.

Lakshmi replied, "An IPS officer and local. Unbending. Not loud like Avaneesh, but he's cleaned up more backroom filth than most DCPs. You'll like him. He listens before he acts."

Naina said in a low voice, "We need someone inside the command structure who can protect Priya. Who can stall a minister's call. Who can move people without alerting the machinery."

Aryan exhaled. "He'll put a target on his own back."

"So did we," Naina said.

Their eyes held for a moment.

Then Aryan looked down at the file again. "Set up the meeting."

Lakshmi nodded. "He'll come to you", she said. "But only once. And only if he senses you're serious."

Aryan muttered, "He'll know."

Because hesitation had no place in the war they were about to start.

***

There was silence in the resort suite.

Naina stood near the balcony, phone in hand, her eyes scanning the trees as if the answer might appear in the shadows. Aryan sat at the small writing desk, refreshing the secure messaging app every few seconds.

"He read it," Aryan said.

Naina didn't turn. "But no reply."

"Which is worse than a 'no'."

"Or smarter than a 'yes'."

They had sent the message through a coded relay—no names, no sender ID, just coordinates, a timestamp, and a phrase Lakshmi told them he'd recognize:

"If the fire touches the boots, do you still walk?"

Aryan leaned back. "Do you think he'll come?" he asked.

Naina finally looked at him. "I think he already has."

He followed her gaze. A lone SUV slowed on the resort's private road, dark grey, with government plates but no escort.

Aryan rose. "Subtle."

Naina grabbed the encrypted drive from the desk. "Hopeful."

A chime sounded on Aryan's phone:

"I will speak. No cameras. No recordings. You get one meeting. Make it matter."

Aryan showed her the message.

She nodded. "He's in."

But neither of them smiled.

Because the game had changed again.

And if Avaneesh Kumar was who Lakshmi believed he was, this wasn't just a meeting; it was the first act of open resistance.

Outside, the SUV pulled into the gravel lot and stopped.

Aryan said, "Let's meet our last line of defence."

***

The door opened without a knock.

Commandant Avaneesh Kumar stepped in, tall, uniformed, his chest a canvas of ribbons earned in places no one dared talk about. His expression gave away nothing.

Aryan stood up instinctively. Naina set the encrypted drive on the table without a word.

Avaneesh scanned the room once, then nodded. "No devices. No chatter. Just facts."

Aryan gestured to the seat opposite him. "We've got plenty of those."

Avaneesh didn't sit. "Then make them count," he said.

Naina spoke first. "We have proof not just of financial misappropriation but also of human trafficking disguised under medical logistics. Vikram Sharma is the bridge. He's protected."

Avaneesh clasped his hands behind his back. "I'm aware of Sharma. And I've suspected his reach. But suspicion isn't enough."

Aryan slid the drive forward. "This is. Timelines. Account trails. Organ transport logs. NGO-backed clearances."

Avaneesh looked down at the drive, then back at Aryan. "And why me?"

"Because you're one of the last who hasn't been compromised," replied Naina.

Silence.

Then the Commandant stepped forward and picked up the drive. He didn't pocket it; he held it like it was more than plastic and data.

"I can't promise protection," he said. "But I can promise a delay. That's all you need, isn't it?"

Aryan nodded. "Just enough space to set fire to the system."

Avaneesh finally sat down.

"Then you've got it."

***

Later that afternoon, the resort's private conference room was repurposed into something far less ceremonial.

Lakshmi Iyer stood by the door as a man entered, no fanfare, no escort, no visible badge. Just pressed khakis, a simple watch, and a steady gaze that scanned the room with silent authority.

DCP Rajesh Kumar.

Aryan rose slightly but didn't extend his hand yet. Naina observed him closely. The man didn't carry rank the way others did. It sat on him like a second skin, natural, unforced.

Lakshmi spoke first. "He's handled trafficking cases no one talks about, cases that stopped before the headlines began."

Rajesh sat down without waiting for permission. "Lakshmi says you have something real," he said. "Something… actionable."

Naina slid a second copy of the drive forward. "It's the same as what we shared with the Commandant. This one's for you."

Rajesh didn't reach for it immediately. He looked at Aryan and asked, "Do you believe justice is possible here?"

Aryan met his gaze. "I believe silence is no longer an option."

Rajesh nodded once. Then he picked up the drive and placed it in his inside pocket.

"I'll vet it," he said. "Quietly. No paper trail. No questions."

Lakshmi added, "He doesn't play politics."

Rajesh looked at Naina. "I don't play anything. I either act, or I don't."

Aryan's shoulders eased slightly. Naina exhaled without realizing she'd been holding her breath.

In a war built on shadows and silence, they had just found a man who moved like light.

***

The table between them might as well have been a negotiation board, two civilians with proof, two officers with reach, and a conspiracy too large for anyone to hold alone.

Commandant Avaneesh spoke first. "Once this information reaches the wrong desk, everything you're building will collapse. Politicians don't disappear quietly. They bury the noise."

DCP Rajesh added, "And if even one name on that list leaks prematurely, we won't just be facing interference, we'll be facing sanctioned retaliation."

Aryan didn't blink. "That's why you're both here," he said. "We can't risk loose ends. We need containment until exposure."

Naina leaned in. "We're not asking for protection. We're asking for precision. Coordinated leaks. Safe extractions. Legal dead ends closed before they're reopened."

Rajesh considered her words. "You're asking for trust in a system designed to avoid accountability," he said.

Naina replied, "No. We're asking you to bend that system just enough to give the truth a running start."

Avaneesh looked at Aryan. "Are you prepared for what happens if you're wrong about us?" he asked.

Aryan replied without hesitation, "Then we'll burn with the files. But the world will still see the fire."

A long pause followed.

Then Rajesh leaned forward. "I want oversight on any media leak," he said. "If this explodes, I don't want it to be a headline war. I want it to be a conviction."

Naina met his gaze. "Then we're aligned."

Four heads nodded reluctantly, but with purpose.

The alliance was fragile. But it was real. And sometimes, the most fragile alliances drew the bloodiest lines.

***

The resort air grew heavier as dusk settled over the hills. The meeting had ended, the room cleared, but Aryan and Naina lingered in the veranda's quiet shade, watching the trees sway, as if waiting for something to shatter the silence.

Aryan checked his phone again. No alerts. No updates. Just encrypted stillness.

"That calm before it hits," he said.

Naina nodded, arms folded. "We just kicked a hornet's nest tied to three ministries and a criminal network."

Aryan exhaled. "Do you think they'll move tonight?" he asked.

"They won't wait for headlines."

Inside, a waiter crossed the hall with tea that no one had ordered. Aryan's eyes followed him for a beat too long.

"We need to rotate safehouses," he said. "Kabir should never stay in one location more than twelve hours."

"I already sent him new coordinates," Naina replied.

He gave her a sideways glance. "Do you always move two steps ahead?"

She smirked and said, "When you're hunted, you don't run; you redirect."

A car passed slowly near the main gate. Not out of place. But not fast either.

Aryan tapped the railing and said, "They're watching."

"They've been watching," Naina said quietly. "The difference is we're finally worth their attention."

Aryan looked out at the fading light in the sky.

"They're not afraid yet," he said.

Naina answered, "They will be."

And in that moment, the silence became a weapon.

And silence, they knew, was always the last thing before the shot.

***

The private garden behind the villa was dimly lit, tucked between two rows of hedges and a lotus pond. Aryan sat on a stone bench, elbows on knees, eyes on the ground.

Naina arrived with two cups of black coffee, handing one to him without a word. They sat in silence for a long moment, neither filling it with strategy, analysis, or fear.

Just presence.

Aryan finally spoke. "I didn't think they'd agree."

Naina sipped her coffee. "You underestimated the rot," she said. "And the men willing to stop it."

He looked at her. "You always see it first—the weakness, the cracks."

"And you always wait for proof," she replied. "We balance each other."

Aryan gave a small laugh. "That almost sounded romantic."

She looked at him then and asked, "Almost?"

He met her gaze, and for once, didn't deflect. "I don't know what this is," he said. "But I know it's not nothing."

The air between them shifted, thick with memory, risk, and unspoken truths.

Naina set her cup down. "I trust you," she said simply.

It landed heavier than any confession.

Aryan reached for her hand and held it in his own.

"No matter what comes next," he said, "we don't let them divide us."

"They won't," she said softly.

And in that fragile moment, trust was no longer a strategy; it was armour.

***

Rajesh Kumar didn't knock when he re-entered the lounge. His face was as composed as ever, but his eyes had changed.

He held a file in his hand. It wasn't thick, but the weight of it shifted the air.

Aryan and Naina stood up as he approached.

"This came through a contact in the cyber-surveillance wing," Rajesh said. "Someone who owed me a favour. I suggest you sit."

Aryan and Naina exchanged looks and sat down.

Rajesh placed the file on the table and opened it.

Inside were two images, three notations, and a printed name in bold type:

Minister Raghav Deshmukh.

Naina leaned forward. "Cabinet-level?"

Rajesh nodded. "Minister of State for Homeland Security."

Aryan let out a breath. "He chairs oversight for the national police, paramilitary, and digital surveillance arms."

Rajesh added, “And he authorized a recent fund flow disguised as rural health innovation, redirected through three shell NGOs. One of them is Vikram’s.”

Naina asked, “How close are they?”

Rajesh tapped a photo. It showed Vikram and Deshmukh at a closed-door symposium in Geneva.

“Close enough to share offshore accounts. And agendas.”

Aryan sat back, staring at the paper. “This isn’t just about TechNova anymore. Or organs. Or NGOs.”

Rajesh folded his arms. “No. It’s about power. The kind that buys silence, rewrites rules, and erases people.”

For a moment, the room was still.

Then Naina said, “Then we burn louder.”

Aryan nodded. “And higher.”

The lines had redrawn themselves.

And the enemy had a title, one powerful enough to erase entire histories.

***

The room was quiet long after Rajesh had left.

Aryan stood by the window, hands in his pockets, staring out at the twilight. Naina remained seated, her fingers tracing the edge of the file as if memorizing the weight of the truth it held.

“He’s protected at every level,” Aryan finally said. “Deshmukh can shut down the media, block inquiries, erase digital trails…”

“And silence whistleblowers before they take their first breath,” Naina finished.

She looked up. “We’re not dealing with corruption. We’re dealing with infrastructure.”

Aryan turned toward her. “So we take it apart, piece by piece.”

“Or expose it all at once,” she countered.

They both knew what that meant. The risks. The retaliation. The sleepless nights and invisible crosshairs.

But they also knew something else: they weren’t alone anymore.

"That drive," Aryan said, gesturing to the table. "We release it, we implicate a sitting minister. This goes beyond career suicide."

Naina stood up. "We're already past saving careers, Aryan."

He nodded slowly. "Then let's focus on saving what matters."

She stepped closer. "Truth?"

He nodded again. "And the people who still believe in it."

Their hands met again, this time not out of comfort, but clarity.

The mission had shifted from unveiling a crime to confronting a regime. And they were ready.

The whiteboard in the resort's conference suite was soon covered in scribbled arrows, names, acronyms, and underlined circles.

Aryan stood with a marker in hand, pacing slowly. "We control the narrative, we control the pace," he said.

Naina added a note near Minister Deshmukh's name. "No immediate leak," she said. "We test the pipeline first, drop one mid-tier name, track the fallout, measure who moves where."

Aryan nodded. "Pressure the inner ring without triggering the full lockdown."

She circled "Arkaris Holdings". "We leak documents from this shell NGO first, enough to trigger questions in Parliament, not panic in the Cabinet."

Aryan stepped back. "And Priya?"

"She goes dark again," Naina said. "Avaneesh assigns a covert guard. Any noise around her, we abort the whole thing."

Kabir pinged their secure chat: "Media backdoor ready. Waiting for payload."

Naina typed back: "Standby. T-minus forty-eight hours."

Aryan turned to her. "Two days?" he asked.

She met his gaze. "That's enough time to alert global allies. If we go loud, we don't go alone."

He set the marker down. "And Vikram?"

Naina's voice lowered. "He's not just a threat. He's bait. Let him believe we're bluffing. Then pull the floor from under him."

A beat passed.

They stood in front of the board, no longer drowning in possibilities but charting their siege.

This wasn't panic; this was planning.

***

The bags were packed, the encrypted drives were secured, and the last traces on the whiteboard were wiped clean.

Aryan handed the keys of the suite to the front desk with a smile that didn't reach his eyes. Naina waited by the car, sunglasses on despite the late hour, her phone vibrating with muted updates.

The sun dipped low behind the hills as they pulled out of the driveway, silence settling in the car.

"Are you sure we left no trail?" Aryan asked after a while.

Naina replied without looking up. "Lakshmi paid in cash. No names. No CCTV. No room records."

Aryan glanced in the rearview mirror. "And the officers?"

"Gone before sunrise," she said. "Like smoke."

They merged onto the highway. The city skyline emerged in the distance, no longer a backdrop, but a battlefield.

Aryan tightened his grip on the wheel. "Two days. Then it all goes live."

Naina nodded. "Kabir has the release nodes programmed," she replied. "Every file is mirrored three times. Even if we disappear, the truth won't."

They didn't speak for a moment.

A truck passed on their left, honking once. Aryan changed lanes without a word.

Then Naina added, "We've never been this exposed."

Aryan replied, "We've also never been this ready."

Because this time, although the road ahead was long, their fear had been replaced by something colder—a resolve and purpose.

***

Later that night, the safehouse was still.

Aryan was asleep on the couch, a jacket draped over him, the exhaustion of the day finally claiming his defiance. Outside, the rain tapped gently against the windowpane like a clock ticking.

Naina sat alone at the kitchen table, laptop open, the screen casting a pale light across her face. She wasn't reading any of the active case files; she was looking at the encrypted folder, the one Kabir had flagged but hadn't yet cracked: "Phoenix-Red: Foreign Relay Unknown."

No sender. No location. Just a timestamp from three months ago. Before the data breach. Before Priya. Before everything.

She didn't move, her thoughts spinning quieter than her breath.

Who else knew?

Who else was already playing this game before they even saw the board?

Aryan stirred on the couch.

Naina stood up and looked out the window at the sleeping city, her eyes narrowing as a streetlight flickered once, then stabilized. "This isn't just ours anymore," she whispered to herself. Then she added, "And it never was." She pulled a blanket over Aryan and sat back down, the encrypted drive still glowing faintly on the table beside her.

They were ready for war.

But the battlefield was far bigger than they thought.

And somewhere beyond the visible lines, older wars still raged in silence.

***

Chapter 9

THE SHATTERED FIREWALL

The data breach report pulsed ominously on Aryan's tablet, its red-highlighted lines blinking like a silent alarm. He paced the length of his office, every footfall echoing off the marble as if mocking his rising anger.

He had built TechNova on precision, foresight, and trust.

And now a leak. From inside.

His fingers clenched the edge of the tablet. "No mistakes," he muttered to himself. "Not at this level."

The office, normally a space of clarity and control, now felt suffocating. Beyond the glass windows, the Mumbai skyline glittered in the distance, oblivious to the fact that one of its most celebrated tech leaders was on the verge of being unravelled.

He tossed the tablet on his desk. It skidded across the surface and came to rest beside an encrypted hard drive, untouched.

Everything he'd worked for, every proprietary file, whistleblower archive, and digital trail, was now vulnerable.

The door to his office slid open with a soft swish.

Aryan didn't turn.

"I know it was you," he said flatly, eyes locked on the city below.

Behind him, silence. Then footsteps.

Rajeev's voice was quiet but strained. "Aryan..."

"Don't," Aryan snapped, finally facing him. "Just tell me it wasn't you."

But the guilt in Rajeev's eyes was louder than any denial.

Aryan's voice was quieter now but sharper. "I trusted you with everything, not just the tech but also the vision, the people."

Rajeev stood near the door, hands stiff by his sides. "I didn't mean for it to go this far."

"You didn't mean to compromise our core server?" Aryan snapped. "You didn't mean to leak classified trails linked to Vikram's funding shells?"

Rajeev winced but didn't answer.

Aryan stepped forward, anger rising behind his measured tone. "You were in the loop on every firewall, every vault. You had access; only four people on this planet did."

Rajeev tried to speak. "Aryan"

"You looked me in the eye last week and told me our systems were solid."

"They were…"

"Then why is my backup server pinging from an offshore proxy with a timestamp linked to your login?"

Silence.

Aryan's chest heaved. He wasn't just angry; he was wounded. Betrayal, when it came from a stranger, stung. But when it came from someone who'd once toasted to your dream...

"I need the truth, Rajeev," he said finally. "Not for protocol. Not for damage control. For me."

Because sometimes truth was the last fragile thing a friendship could save.

Rajeev looked up, and Aryan saw not defiance but fear in his face.

Not for himself. For someone else. Rajeev sank into the chair across from Aryan, as if finally letting the weight drop from his shoulders.

"They threatened my daughter," he said. No buildup. No preamble. Just the truth.

Aryan's breath caught.

"They knew her school," said Rajeev hopelessly. "Her route home. Even what flavour of ice cream she buys on Wednesdays. Vikram's people. Or whoever's running his back end."

He rubbed his hands together, knuckles white, and continued, "One night, there was a picture in my inbox of her getting into my wife's car. Time-stamped. GPS-tagged."

Aryan stood frozen, his anger slowly receding under something colder. "And they said what? 'Send the files or we take her'?" he asked.

Rajeev nodded. "They didn't need to say it outright. I knew what they meant. I stalled as long as I could. But then... they gave me the file names, specific ones. I copied them, sent them out through a dummy relay, and deleted every trace."

He looked up, tears now threatening the corners of his eyes. "I didn't know what was in them, Aryan. I didn't look. I just wanted them to stop watching her."

Aryan turned away, jaw clenched.

This wasn't the betrayal of a spy or saboteur. This was the betrayal of a father backed into a corner.

And some corners left no honourable way out.

Naina entered quietly, her eyes scanning the room, catching the shift in energy.

Rajeev looked at her, voice barely holding. "I'm sorry. I didn't know what else to do."

Aryan didn't speak. He just walked to the far corner of the room and rested both palms against the glass wall, staring out at the distant skyline. His reflection in the pane was dim, fractured, like the version of himself that trusted without question.

Rajeev's voice still lingered in the air: "I just wanted them to stop watching her."

Naina stood silently near the desk, arms crossed, absorbing the moment like a pressure gauge reading a system on the verge of blowing.

Aryan finally spoke, his voice low. "I brought him into this. Gave him clearance. Let him into every encrypted channel because I believed in loyalty."

"He didn't betray you," Naina said, quietly but firmly. "He protected his daughter."

Aryan turned slowly. His eyes weren't angry anymore, just tired. "And in doing that, he may have exposed every name we're trying to protect."

Rajeev said nothing. He sat still, his head bowed in shame.

Aryan ran a hand through his hair, pacing in short bursts. "I would've done the same," he said. "God help me, I would've done the exact same thing."

Naina stepped closer. "Then maybe this isn't about blame anymore. Maybe it's about course correction."

Aryan met her gaze. No resistance. Just a man stripped of illusion, standing in the ruins of his own certainty.

The silence held for a beat longer before Naina crossed the room with quiet precision and stood in front of Rajeev.

"Who contacted you?" she asked. Her tone wasn't angry. It was exact.

Rajeev blinked, unprepared for the pivot. "I… I don't know the real name," he said. "Just an encrypted email. No signature. The first message came through a disposable relay account—masked IP."

"Did they ever speak to you directly?" she asked.

He shook his head. "Only text. Always cold. Efficient. Like a script."

"Did they ask for anything other than files?"

"No. Just specific folders. Internal QA logs. Off-record audit trails. And two encrypted vault references. I thought they just wanted leverage, not... whatever this really is."

Naina exchanged a look with Aryan. "Those folders contained the pilot patient IDs and the raw biometric stream," she said. "It's not just leverage; it's traceable proof of human testing without clearance."

Rajeev paled.

Naina continued, unflinching. "How did you transmit the data?"

"A secure drive. I uploaded through a ghosted private server. The port closed ninety seconds after the transfer."

"Did you keep any logs? Any trace?"

"I deleted everything."

She paused, then said in a clipped voice, "Next time, you leave breadcrumbs. Because if we're going to survive this, we'll need to burn their trail louder than they can burn ours." Rajeev just nodded.

Aryan watched, saying nothing.

Because in that moment, Naina wasn't just leading; she was shielding them both. Rajeev's hands trembled slightly as he reached into his coat pocket and pulled out a small envelope. He passed it to Aryan without a word.

Inside were printed photographs. Personal. Targeted.

Aryan flipped through them slowly—Rajeev's daughter at her school gate, his wife shopping at a local market. The timestamp on one photo was just three days old.

"They weren't bluffing," Rajeev said, his voice raw. "They knew every movement, every routine. I called the police quietly. But there was nothing actionable. No licence-plate, no faces. Just pressure."

Naina's jaw tightened, but she didn't speak.

Rajeev looked at Aryan. "I thought I could hold them off with time. But the moment they mentioned my daughter by name... I broke."

Aryan didn't move.

He was seeing more than a friend.

He was seeing a father who had tried to outplay monsters with borrowed minutes and failed.

Rajeev added, "They never wanted money, just access. It wasn't blackmail for profit; it was for silence. And I gave it to them."

Naina stepped in. "You didn't give them silence," she said gently. "You gave them a crack in the wall. But we can seal it. If we're smart."

Rajeev's eyes were glassy. "If she ever gets hurt..."

"She won't," Aryan said quietly.

For the first time since the confrontation began, his voice wasn't hard. It was steady. Determined.

Because now he understood.

This wasn't war with soldiers; it was war with a father.

Aryan glanced at Naina, and she nodded, barely but firmly. In that instant, something shifted. Not forgiveness, not entirely. But clarity. They didn't have time to fall apart.

He turned back to Rajeev, his voice measured. "What's done is done. We don't bury mistakes. We repurpose them."

Rajeev's head lifted, surprised. "You're not cutting me out?"

Aryan shook his head. "Not yet. You know the system better than anyone. You also know how it can be broken."

Naina stepped forward. "We've sealed the primary breach," she said. "Now we focus on containment. You're going to help us map every node your data might've touched, server-side, relay-side, and dark web hits. No gaps."

Rajeev nodded slowly, the burden still heavy but now carried with direction.

Aryan walked to the window and stared at the skyline again. It looked different this time, more fragile, more real.

He said softly, "The moment we let fear divide us, Vikram wins. Every single time. And division was Vikram's favourite weapon."

Naina added, "And the moment we stand still, someone else falls."

The room didn't relax, but it steadied.

Rajeev wiped his eyes and stood up straight.

No apologies. No promises.

Just a quiet agreement—move forward or be swallowed.

Aryan turned back to his console. "Let's get to work."

***

Naina stood in front of the master terminal, her fingers already dancing across the keyboard. Rajeev and Aryan watched as layers of code folded and refolded, silent shields rebuilding in real-time.

"The first priority," she said, "is to mirror all critical assets to an air-gapped vault. No cloud sync. No automated backups."

Aryan leaned over her shoulder. "What about the surveillance relays?"

"Already dead," she replied. "Killed them while you were staring out the window."

Rajeev raised an eyebrow. "Do you always move this fast?" he asked.

Naina didn't look up. "Only when we're bleeding."

She opened a sub-routine titled 'EchoGlass', a honeypot firewall that mimicked their real server structure.

"They'll think they're still in," she explained. "But what they're watching is a mirrored sandbox. Every file they access will ping their location."

Aryan exhaled. "Reverse surveillance."

Naina smirked. "We learned from the best."

Rajeev looked from one to the other and asked, "What do you need from me?"

Naina paused, then turned to him. "Audit your past six months of login paths," she said. "Flag every third-party API call you didn't initiate. I want IP stamps, time logs, shadow directories, everything."

Rajeev nodded and sat at the side terminal.

Aryan watched her as she worked, focused, fearless, fluent in the language of digital war.

This time, they weren't reacting; they were hunting.

They weren't just plugging holes; they were laying traps. For once, the predators would be the prey.

The room hummed with the soft rhythm of keystrokes and encrypted data transfer. Outside, the skyline was slowly darkening, but inside, momentum was building.

Aryan stepped away from the central terminal and turned to Rajeev. "There's something you can do," he said.

Rajeev looked up, hopeful but wary.

Aryan tossed him a small, black, unmarked drive, cold to the touch. "This is a custom sandbox node. It's not traceable, not logged in our system. It holds a decoy variant of the Mediscan data, scrubbed but dressed up to look authentic."

Rajeev frowned. "You want me to… feed them this?"

Aryan nodded. "Use the same upload path they gave you. Make them believe they're still in control."

Rajeev hesitated, then asked apprehensively, "What if they trace it back to me again?"

Aryan didn't flinch. "They already know who you are. What matters now is making them think you're still theirs."

Naina added, "This buys us two things: time and attention. While they're decrypting garbage, we reposition our assets."

Rajeev looked down at the drive in his hand, as if it might burn him. “You’re trusting me with this?” he asked.

“No,” Aryan said. “I’m giving you the chance to earn it back.”

A long pause ensued. Then Rajeev stood up and slid the drive into his jacket. “I won’t let you down again.”

Aryan looked at him. “Don’t let her down,” he said in a quiet voice.

Rajeev nodded, understanding exactly who he meant.

The atmosphere in the room had shifted. It wasn’t warm, but it wasn’t fractured anymore either. It was functionally focused, like survivors who had found rhythm again in the wreckage.

Aryan checked the sync logs on the backup drives. “Vault A is locked,” he said. “Full integrity check verified.”

Naina, seated at the operations console, scanned the threat matrix. “Two possible shadows left behind,” she said. “I’m scrubbing one now, the other’s ghosting a French server farm. Kabir can tail it.”

Rajeev updated the timeline board on the wall, using coloured markers for breach windows, log trails, and mirror decoys. His movements were slower than Naina’s and less confident than Aryan’s, but deliberate.

They weren’t a flawless team, but they were a functioning one. Aryan glanced at the clock, 23:17.

“We’ve got six hours before the dummy relay activates,” he said. “We’ll need to be off-grid by then.”

Naina stood up, stretching her arms. “I’ve already booked three safe locations under rotated IDs. No one sleeps in the same place twice.”

Rajeev looked up. “What about Kabir?”

“He’s mobile,” Aryan said. “Which means safer than us.”

There was no small talk. No wasted energy. Every gesture served the next step.

But even in the silence, something else was growing—trust, forged not in certainty, but in necessity.

As Aryan looked at both of them, he realized something strange.

For the first time since this began, they weren’t reacting.

They were finally leading.

***

The tension in the room had cooled to a quiet hum. Not gone, just better managed.

Aryan reviewed the alert logs one more time, then muttered under his breath, "If one more ghost IP pings this grid, I'm personally writing code in Sanskrit."

Naina, hunched over a terminal, smirked. "You'd misspell your own name in Devanagari."

Rajeev looked up, puzzled. "Wait, you know Sanskrit?"

Aryan turned to him, deadpan. "I know how to pretend I do, which is 90 per cent of corporate leadership."

For a second, all three paused, then, almost unexpectedly, a small ripple of laughter broke out.

Not loud. Not careless.

But real.

It was the first time they'd laughed together in weeks.

Naina leaned back in her chair, arms crossed loosely. "Don't get too relaxed," she said. "The last time you joked mid-crisis, we ended up running through an underground parking garage with a hard drive taped to a coffee cup."

Aryan smiled faintly. "And it worked."

Rajeev chuckled. "God, I miss boring meetings."

Naina raised an eyebrow. "We'll earn one. After we burn this empire down."

Aryan nodded, still smiling. "Tea. Laughter. Prison sentences in sealed envelopes. The usual."

But between jokes, they remembered the war was still waging.

It was a fleeting moment, but it was a necessary reminder that beyond the code, the politics, and the fallout, they were still people.

And people needed reasons to keep fighting.

Even if it was just for one more bad joke between battles.

***

The moment passed.

Laughter gave way to silence as Rajeev froze at his console, eyes narrowing at something scrolling across the screen.

Aryan noticed first. “What is it?”

Rajeev didn’t answer immediately. He expanded the window, filtering through terminal commands and trace logs. His voice dropped. “There’s a second signal.”

Naina was standing behind him in seconds. “From where?” she asked.

“Not Vikram’s usual grid. This one’s bouncing off a masked node out of the eastern Seaboard, routing through two inactive government contractor domains.”

Aryan leaned in. “Which departments?”

Rajeev clicked through layers of metadata. “One is flagged under health innovation,” he replied. “The other looks like a dormant Ministry of Communications project.”

Naina’s tone sharpened. “That’s not a shell. That’s a cover.”

Aryan’s jaw tightened. “So this isn’t just Vikram’s private blackmail racket. It’s institutional.”

Rajeev nodded slowly. “And whoever they are… they’re watching us watch them. This isn’t passive surveillance. It’s recursive.”

Aryan straightened. “Which means we just stared too long into the abyss, and it stared back.”

Naina whispered, “Deshmukh.”

Aryan met her eyes. “Or someone above him.”

The screen flashed once—an auto-wipe sequence was trying to self-initiate.

Rajeev slammed a kill-switch key. “Got it. I blocked the wipe. We still have a copy.”

Aryan exhaled. “Then we’re not just fighting corruption anymore.”

Naina replied, her voice cold and clear, “We’re in a shadow war, one where truth wears masks and silence carries knives.”

***

The sun was beginning to rise, casting a muted golden hue across the skyline. But inside the safehouse, the war-room energy hadn't dimmed.

Aryan stood in front of the strategy board, now cluttered with colour-coded markers, digital maps, and layered signal paths.

"The tech conference buys us two things," he said. "Visibility and time."

Rajeev adjusted the digital relay graph. "I've created a parallel broadcast signal. If anything goes wrong during your keynote, the data goes live automatically."

Naina nodded, already running the public escalation script from her secure tablet. "I'll plant the payload behind Aryan's presentation file," she said. "It won't trigger unless someone tampers with it. If Vikram moves... the truth detonates."

Aryan looked at her, quietly impressed. "Fail-safe inside a fail-safe."

"After what we've seen," she replied, "we don't get second chances."

The trio worked like gears clicking in place, moving in rhythm.

Passwords confirmed. Access credentials re-verified. Decoy packets loaded. The pressure was real, but so was the precision.

The hours ahead would decide whether they remained rebels or became martyrs. Rajeev checked the backup alert protocol. "We'll need to rotate communications every three hours. No open channels. No shared files."

Aryan agreed. "Everyone speaks in layers. Everyone watches everyone."

The clock on the wall ticked louder than before.

In twenty-four hours, they would walk into the lion's den.

Not to beg. But to light a match.

***

The operations room had quietened.

Most of the screens were dark now, save for a single terminal pulsing a faint blue, running silent diagnostics. The storm of crisis had passed for the moment. In its place was a stillness that felt earned.

Rajeev had gone to the adjoining room to rest. Aryan stood on the balcony, one hand on the railing, the city lights twinkling in the distance like a sky turned upside down.

Naina joined him silently, her presence calm, anchoring.

He didn't turn. "You should get some sleep."

"So should you," she replied.

He nodded slowly, his eyes never leaving the city's skyline. "Do you think we'll make it through this?"

Naina leaned beside him, arms folded. "That depends."

"On what?"

"On whether we still have something to come back to when this ends."

He looked at her then and asked, "Do we?"

She didn't answer right away.

Then she said softly, "We might. If we don't let this war consume all of us."

They stood in silence again, the kind that carried weight but also understanding.

Aryan reached for her hand, hesitated for half a second, then took it.

She didn't pull away.

Their fingers intertwined, wordless but sure.

Not surrender. Not escape. Just a connection. They stood in silence. For a brief, fragile moment, it felt like time had paused long enough to breathe, to hope, to feel.

Then Aryan's encrypted device buzzed once in his pocket.

He glanced at the screen. The alert was from Priya, urgent, top priority.

Naina noticed the change in his expression immediately. "What is it?" she asked.

Aryan handed her the device. The message was simple but chilling:

"Warehouse location confirmed. Victims inside. Human trafficking verified. Movement expected tonight. Clock's ticking."

Naina exhaled, sharp and slow. "So it's real."

Aryan nodded. "She looped in Avaneesh and Rajesh," he said. "The command team's mobilizing now."

He looked at her, reluctant to let the moment pass, yet knowing it must. "We don't get to pause long, do we?"

Naina's hand slipped from his, not in rejection but in readiness. "We'll pause when they're safe."

Aryan stepped back inside, already reaching for his communications gear. "I'll alert Kabir. You coordinate the tactical links."

"I'm on it," she said, her voice clear and focused now.

Their eyes met again, something exchanged, something understood.

The moment of peace was over.

War had called them back.

And neither of them would turn away because some battles demanded more than courage. They demanded the surrender of fear itself.

***

Chapter 10

NO SILENCE, NO SURRENDER

The alley was cloaked in darkness, the kind that swallowed noise and magnified tension. Aryan crouched beside a rusted dumpster, scanning the perimeter of the warehouse through night-vision lenses.

Naina knelt beside him, calm and composed, her tablet casting a soft green glow on her face. She was already running thermal overlays and digital blueprints of the building. "Two guards at the south exit," she said in a low voice. "One patrol inside, east corridor. Cameras are wired to a private loop."

Aryan nodded. "Any blind spots?"

"North side, top level. There's a broken camera and a rusted ventilation shaft. Small, but usable. If we scale the adjacent wall, we can drop into the admin office."

He smirked. "Remind me to never bet against your route-mapping skills."

"Betting against me was never your strong suit," she countered.

Aryan's smile faded as he surveyed the structure again. "Do you think Vikram's still using this site personally?"

Naina shrugged. "He may have moved on. But if even half the data we pulled from Rajeev's dummy drive is real, there's something big here. Victims. Paper trails. Maybe even digital backups."

Footsteps crunched on gravel behind them. It was Priya.

"Backup's two minutes out," she said. "Rajesh is sweeping the perimeter with his team. Avaneesh wants your word before breaching."

Aryan stood, adjusting the communications unit on his collar. "Then let's give him the green light."

Naina glanced at the structure once more. "This time," she said, "we don't just expose a system. We dismantle it because justice wasn't enough anymore. Justice needed to roar."

Aryan nodded. "One floor at a time."

Priya adjusted the strap on her tactical vest as she joined Aryan and Naina behind the loading bay wall. The gravity in her eyes said everything. This wasn't just another operation; it was personal.

"They're moving people tonight," she said quietly. "My source inside said two trucks have already left. If we don't act now, the rest will vanish before dawn."

Naina's brows furrowed. "How many inside?"

"Seventeen confirmed. Mostly women. Two minors. Medical files suggest they were prepped for international transport, organ prep, sedation logs, and digital tags."

Aryan's jaw tightened. "Time?"

"Thirty minutes. Maybe less."

Footsteps approached. It was Commandant Avaneesh Kumar, flanked by DCP Rajesh Kumar. Both officers wore no-nonsense expressions and carried the weight of their uniforms like it was armour.

Avaneesh gave a curt nod. "We've secured the north and west exits. No movement yet."

Rajesh added, "No sign of external interference. But we'll need to move fast once the breach begins."

Aryan turned to Naina. "You'll lead the digital blackout. Disable cameras, mute alarms, kill trackers."

Naina was already pulling up her interface. "Running a false loop now," she said. "You'll have an eight-minute window before the system realizes the feed's on a loop."

Priya checked her watch. "That's all we need."

The group exchanged a silent glance, professional, focused, united.

Avaneesh's voice cut through the quiet. "Let's bring them out alive."

Aryan exhaled slowly. "Let's bring them all home. Every heartbeat beyond those walls deserves a second chance."

And just like that, the mission had begun.

Inside the darkened operations van, a schematic diagram of the warehouse glowed across the tablet screens. Aryan stood beside Avaneesh and Rajesh, while Naina synced their communication frequencies.

"We move in three squads," Avaneesh said. "Alpha breaches the north wall: three men, two medics, one extraction lead."

Rajesh pointed at the eastern corridor. "Bravo secures the holding zone. That's where they'll keep the women and minors. Clean sweep, zero aggression unless provoked."

Aryan added, "I'll move with Alpha. Naina will run silent surveillance and system disruption from the field hub."

Naina shot him a look. "You're not getting shot today, Mehra. Stay behind the front line."

Aryan smirked. "You've said that before."

Rajesh clicked his communication unit into place. "Once we breach, no verbal chatter. Silent markers only. Hand signals if needed. Priya's unit handles trauma response."

Avaneesh addressed the team through the open van door. "Minimal force. Prioritize safety. No glory. No delay."

There was a short silence.

Then Aryan turned to the group and said, "This is our line. Right here. We cross it together, and we walk everyone back."

He met Naina's eyes, calm, sharp, grounded.

Rajesh pulled his gloves on. "Then let's make history."

The back doors swung open. Outside, Bangalore slept, unaware that, in the shadow of warehouses and whispered crimes, a rescue mission was ready to strike.

***

The mobile command van was a hive of motion. Inside, tactical maps lit the walls while three separate communication channels crackled in low sync.

Commandant Avaneesh Kumar stood over the digital schematic diagram, laser-focused. "Alpha Unit, position north and west flank. Bravo, hold south access. You see movement, you don't act unless I say. Copy?"

His CRPF team responded in clipped tones, already dispersing into the night.

Aryan zipped his tactical vest as Naina rechecked her override jammers. Rajesh snapped shut his sidearm holster, then joined them near the secondary van door.

"Perimeter sealed," Rajesh reported. "Two entry points under surveillance. Primary breach team is you, me, and CRPF Commando Pair One."

Avaneesh looked up. "Rao, can you scramble their wireless channel for 10 minutes?"

Naina didn't flinch. "Twelve, if they're still using the eastern grid protocol."

He gave a faint nod. "You'll have ghost cover. After that, if we're not out, burn the route."

Aryan met Avaneesh's gaze. "No one left behind."

Avaneesh nodded again. "That includes you," he said.

Outside, boots crunched. The team moved like vapour, dispersed but synchronized. Aryan could tell this wasn't their first night raid.

Rajesh raised a hand. "Two minutes."

Avaneesh gave the final order. "My team shadows yours from 40 metres. No engagement unless backup is called. Rajesh, Aryan, you lead the door. I cover the flank."

Aryan glanced at Naina.

"Let's go."

The operation unfolded in a precision silence only seasoned units could maintain.

Avaneesh's CRPF commandos moved like shadows, securing the perimeter and relaying flank updates through hand signals. One team peeled toward the eastern boundary wall. Another group took overwatch positions from an adjacent rooftop, rifles scanning the windows for any heat bloom or movement.

Aryan crouched behind a storage crate near the north entrance, Rajesh beside him. Two CRPF commandos were positioned behind them, lean, black-suited, night-vision-ready.

"Entry camera loops are stable," Naina whispered through the communication channel. "You've got ten minutes before the system clocks the ghost feed."

Rajesh raised a closed fist. The team froze.

Avaneesh's voice came low over the alternate channel. "South alley clear. One possible observer near the generator that our unit will handle. Proceed."

A commando moved forward, disabling the lock with a silent tool kit. The metal door gave way with a slow groan. Aryan stepped in, followed by Rajesh and the flanking CRPF duo.

The air inside the warehouse was stale, heavy with machinery oil and something else—something human.

Over the communication channels, Avaneesh marked movement: "Internal heat signature stationary, east corridor. Patrol pattern suggests routine. He won't spot you unless you rush the next corner."

Aryan gave a hand signal.

They advanced with precision.

One commando signalled from behind a cargo unit—cleared.

Rajesh whispered, "This corridor splits. Holding cells should be to the west."

Naina confirmed, "Thermals suggest six to eight signatures, low movement. That's your cluster."

The mission had begun, not just with force, but with foresight.

And Commandant Avaneesh was right where he belonged—in the fight.

The door to the west wing creaked open with measured force. Rajesh moved first, sweeping left with torchlight angled downward. Behind him, Aryan and the two CRPF commandos covered the right arc, rifles ready, breath measured.

The interior holding cell was stark, with bare flooring, metal walls, and fluorescent lights that blinked with a sickly rhythm.

Eight figures huddled in the corners. Women, mostly. Two teenage girls. One child, barely awake, curled into a pile of torn blankets. No one screamed. They simply looked up, silent, stunned.

Aryan's throat tightened. These were not just entries on a tablet or lines in a logbook.

They were people.

Behind them, Priya's voice came through the communication channel. "Medic team entering west corridor. Five seconds out."

The door slid open again, and Priya entered with two medics and an oxygen bag. One CRPF commando moved to secure the adjoining hallway, silently signalling an all-clear.

Rajesh stepped forward, kneeling in front of a shivering girl. "You're safe now," he said gently. "We're getting you out."

Aryan moved to a boy. His eyes were wide but clear, like he had already processed fear and now simply waited.

Aryan offered him a hand. The boy took it.

Outside, Avaneesh's voice came through the channel: "Southern alley clear. One perimeter camera failed to reset from the field console. No hostilities in sight."

Naina's voice came in. "New thermal ping near rear fenceis a false alarm. Rat-sized. Carry on."

The team exhaled but didn't slow.

Because this was the moment they had trained for.

And no one would be left behind.

"Go," Aryan said softly.

Rajesh gave the signal, and the team moved silently, synchronized and surgical.

Two CRPF commandos took point, clearing the left corridor. Another pair formed a moving wall behind the medics and the rescued victims. Avaneesh, monitoring from the outer perimeter, coordinated their progress with the precision of battlefield chess.

"Team Bravo, eyes on west gate. Alpha, shift 10 metres south. Extract unit inbound," Avaneesh ordered.

Aryan guided the boy and two young women forward, his hand steady at their backs. Rajesh assisted an older woman with bruised arms and distant eyes. Priya and the medics carried hydration packs, calming murmurs following them like a blanket.

Outside, the secondary extraction vehicles waited in blackout formation. Naina, from her fixed cover point, tracked movement across the thermal grid.

"Route Delta is clean. Southern guard rotation is thirty seconds off. If you move now, you make it."

Avaneesh's voice cut in immediately. "Copy that. Mobile units sweep flank five. No missed exits. Let nothing bleed through the edges."

The first evacuation van rolled forward. The boy looked out the window, then up at Aryan. He didn't say thank you. He didn't need to. He held Aryan's hand like it was the only thing keeping him tethered to the earth. In a world that had abandoned them, this small kindness was rebellion.

One by one, they loaded.

Two lives at a time.

Each step was heavier than the last but also lighter than the moment before.

This was more than rescue. It was reckoning.

***

Naina's fingers flew across her tablet. The extraction was ahead of schedule—three vans loaded, rear path stable, thermal scans still quiet.

Then a heat signature flickered into view near the alley gate, lone, pacing, erratic.

She zoomed in. Civilian clothes. Limping gait. Cuffed shirt sleeves.

"Unidentified on east perimeter," she whispered. "No CRPF tag. Pattern irregular. Solo, no known patrol alignment."

Aryan's voice tightened in her ear. "Visual confirm?"

She cursed under her breath. "It's Sharma."

Inside the communications van, Avaneesh stood straight, watching the same feed through an auxiliary link.

"Sharma?" he repeated. "He wasn't cleared for field observation."

Rajesh's voice cut in. "If he sees the evacuation…"

"I'm on it," Naina said.

Avaneesh snapped into motion. "Echo-Three, standby intercept position. Shadow him. No contact unless he crosses secure lane. We don't escalate unless forced."

His commando team melted into position, silent phantoms positioning behind Sharma's blind spots, waiting.

Meanwhile, Naina slid into the alley, phone to ear, her voice sharp with faux frustration. "Hello? GPS says I'm still in Koramangala. I'm standing next to a dumpster!"

Sharma blinked, caught off-guard.

"Ma'am," he said, stepping forward, failing to see her clearly in the dark. "You're in a restricted..."

"Do I look like I'm running a raid? I just wanted signal and a shortcut!" Naina fumed into her phone.

Behind Sharma, the final van pulled into motion.

Naina locked eyes with one of the CRPF shadows, who gave a slow blink, clear.

The last survivor was gone.

And Sharma never even knew.

The last extraction van cleared the alley. Its tail lights blinked once, then disappeared behind the ridge of parked cargo trucks.

Mission complete. From the rooftop across the street, a CRPF overwatch operative tapped twice on his microphone. **All clear.**

Naina backed out of the alley, maintaining her flustered civilian act until she rounded the corner and slipped behind a loading crate. She exhaled sharply.

"Visual obstruction cleared," she whispered. "Sharma's none the wiser."

Inside the communications van, Avaneesh gave a slow nod and commanded:

"All units, peel back. Sweep and vanish."

On cue, his commandos vanished from sight, dropping from ledges, slipping through shadows, disappearing like smoke. They left nothing behind. No shells, no prints, no digital dust.

Rajesh, already in the second support vehicle, checked in. "All detainees secured. Priya confirms stable vitals on all eight. No threats en route."

Aryan stood just outside the main gate, his figure etched against the silence of victory.

He looked up toward the rooftop where Avaneesh's sniper had been stationed.

It was now empty. Not a whisper. Not a trace. Just the feeling of something immense having passed.

Aryan clicked his communication unit one last time. "To all units, thank you. We brought them home."

Avaneesh's voice came back, low, composed, resolute.

"No applause. No attention. Just one less warehouse."

And then his voice was gone.

Just as he had arrived.

Like a soldier who didn't need the world to know he'd been there.

The last of the convoy disappeared into the mist of dawn, tail lights blinking. The operation had ended without a single casualty.

But it didn't feel like victory.

Aryan stood near the rear of the extraction van, watching Priya tend to the rescued women now bundled in thermal blankets. The young boy clutched a juice packet with both hands like it was gold.

Rajesh was on the phone, quietly updating headquarters. Avaneesh gave his standby men the stand-down signal, his expression unreadable.

Naina approached silently, peeling off her gloves. Her eyes scanned the scene, not like an operator, but like someone taking stock of the human cost.

"They're safe," Aryan said, almost to himself.

She stopped beside him. "Yes. But that's not the same as being free."

He nodded, absorbing her words.

Their eyes followed Priya as she crouched beside one of the younger girls, smiling at her gently. The girl blinked, then leaned into the touch.

That was freedom, too, earned moment by moment.

Aryan exhaled. "You kept us together back there," he said.

Naina shook her head. "We kept each other steady."

They shared a glance, full of unspoken words, trust, and exhaustion. There was no need for flair or summary.

"Come on," Aryan said after a pause. "Let's disappear before the press catches wind of this."

Naina smiled faintly. "For once, I wouldn't mind disappearing."

***

A few hours later, they gathered at a secure location on the outskirts of the city, an abandoned training compound retrofitted for digital forensics. The concrete walls hummed with routers and fan-cooled processors.

Rajeev sat at the centre console, sifting through the cloned data pulled from the warehouse server. His fingers moved fast, but his eyes mirrored the gravity of what he was seeing.

Aryan stood behind him, arms crossed. "Anything actionable?"

Rajeev nodded grimly. "Plenty. Ledger logs, transport manifests, shipment routes masked as NGO exports. They weren't just trafficking people. They were laundering bio-data."

Naina asked, "Biometric scans?"

Rajeev clicked open a cluster of files. "Eye scans, fingerprints, even DNA samples tagged by blood group and risk index. They were building predictive health profiles."

Aryan's voice turned hard. "For clients?"

"Private clinics. Possibly pharmaceutical research. All offshore."

Avaneesh frowned. "This isn't black-market trafficking," he said. "It's data-driven exploitation."

Rajesh added, "And if these profiles fall into political hands..."

Naina completed the sentence. "It's surveillance by another name. Targeted manipulation."

A long silence followed.

Aryan leaned closer to the screen. "Tag everything," he said. "Encrypt it. Then prepare two copies, one for the court, one for insurance."

Priya, standing at the back, looked shaken. "We thought we were dealing with criminals. But this…"

Aryan's eyes never left the monitor. "We're dealing with an industry."

And suddenly, what they'd just survived felt like the surface of something far more dangerous. They hadn't ended the darkness. They had just found its true depths.

The room was silent, the air heavy with what they now knew and what they didn't.

Rajeev leaned back in his chair, rubbing his temples. "We need more than exposés and data leaks," he said. "If this goes deeper, it'll take people down with us. Good people."

Aryan stared at the flickering code on the screen, his mind already mapping the next ten moves.

Priya broke the silence. "Then let them come."

Everyone turned to her.

She stood near the open window, her posture straight despite the exhaustion. "Let them try to bury us in courtrooms and headlines," she said quietly. "We've saved lives tonight. That counts."

Naina gave a slight nod. "It does."

Priya's gaze swept over the room. "They'll spin stories, call it a PR stunt, frame it as a corporate feud," she said. "But what matters is we don't stop. Not until every person in those files is accounted for. Not until Vikram and whoever else is feeding this pipeline is exposed."

Rajesh folded his arms. "So, what's next?"

Aryan's eyes found Naina's.

She met his look with quiet steadiness, then turned to the group. "The tech conference," she said. "We go public. We show proof—controlled, precise, and undeniable."

Aryan added, "No leaks. No spin. We take the stage and make the world look us in the eye."

Priya's voice softened. "Then we'd better make it count."

***

Aryan's phone buzzed on the table beside him. Another press request. Another flood of messages from board members, shareholders, "concerned allies".

Rajeev looked up from his screen. "They're already spinning stories, leaks, counter-leaks, half-truths. They're drowning us in noise before we can act."

Naina crossed her arms, eyes locked on the digital dashboard. "That's the game. If they control the narrative, it doesn't matter how true our files are."

Priya stepped forward. "So we push back," she said. "Broadcast. Leak it first."

Aryan shook his head. "No. If we do that, we lose control. This isn't about exposure. It's about precision."

He met Naina's gaze. "We don't go public," he said. "Not yet. We go quiet and deep. We build a case that can't be spun, one that corners them in their own system."

Naina nodded slowly. "Encrypted drop servers. Verified logs. Layered testimony."

Rajesh added, "And legal liaisons who don't blink at political heat."

Aryan stepped away from the screen, his voice lower now. "We're not here to light a bonfire. We're here to strike a fault line, one that would split the foundations of power in ways that couldn't be ignored."

For a moment, the room stilled.

Then Naina gave a single nod. "Then let's make sure the first crack runs through the centre."

They wouldn't need a stage. Just patience and leverage.

***

The conference buzzed behind them—press badges, name tags, soft music, and polite deception. But Aryan and Naina didn't step on the stage. They didn't need the spotlight.

Instead, they slipped out a side exit, past the rows of white-draped cocktail tables and LED displays. They followed a narrow service staircase that led upward, emerging onto the rooftop terrace.

On the rooftop, the wind blew gently, noise faded. Bangalore stretched below like a breathing circuit board.

"Quite the circus," Aryan muttered, hands in his pockets.

Naina's lips curled. "It's better to be above it than inside it."

He chuckled. "Still good at finding exits."

"Still good at making messes."

They leaned against the railing, letting the wind speak. Below, the city hummed with headlines they'd chosen not to fuel.

Aryan reached into his coat pocket and pulled out a secure flash drive. "I already gave a copy of this to our legal contact at DRC," he said. "One sealed, time-stamped version. No leaks. No drama."

Naina looked at him. "So we wait."

"We don't wait," he said. "We prepare."

This was no victory lap. It was a pause, an exhale between battles.

But it was also something else. Something warmer. Quieter.

The rooftop shimmered with quiet possibility. Bangalore's skyline stretched endlessly beyond them, glittering, breathing, alive. For a long moment, they stood together, the city alive below them, but their world narrowed to this fragile calm.

"I never thanked you," Aryan said, his voice lower now. "For staying. For seeing past what everyone else assumed."

Naina turned to him, her eyes unreadable. "I wasn't just fighting for you."

He looked at her, the corners of his mouth curving upward, not in humour, but in something closer to wonder. "I know."

There was a moment of charged silence. Then, gently, he asked, "Come with me?"

She hesitated for half a second. Then nodded.

The elevator down from the rooftop was private, leading directly into Aryan's penthouse above the venue. With every floor they passed, the air felt heavier, denser. By the time the doors opened, the air between them was thick with anticipation.

The space opened before them: glass, steel, the city beyond. Sleek furnishings and hushed lighting made the room feel more like a memory than a home. Yet, it was exactly that—Aryan's world, redefined by everything they had just survived.

"Welcome to my humble abode," he said with a self-conscious chuckle.

Naina raised a brow. "Humble?"

"Don't judge," he said, moving to the bar. "Do you want a nightcap?"

She nodded. "Please."

They stood before the window, glasses in hand, gazing at the cityscape. Naina sipped slowly. "It's beautiful," she said. "But lonely, I'd imagine."

Aryan met her gaze in the glass. "It has been," he said quietly. "Until now."

She turned toward him.

He set his glass aside.

"What are we doing?" she whispered.

He stepped closer, his voice barely above a breath. "Something we should have done a long time ago."

His hand reached for her face, gentle, unsure, reverent.

Their kiss was slow and deep. There was no need to rush; this was not an escape. This was a discovery. Reclaiming what was once lost, now found again.

Naina's fingers tangled in Aryan's hair. His arms slid around her waist, drawing her into the safety of something that had once been dangerous.

They moved through the penthouse like a memory, undoing each other with touch and truth. Clothes fell away, unhurried. There were no masks here, only breath and skin and years of tension slowly unwinding.

They reached the bed in a cascade of soft laughter and fierce longing.

"You're even more beautiful than I remember," Aryan murmured, brushing hair from her cheek.

"And you're still infuriatingly charming," Naina replied, hands exploring familiar planes, finding comfort in the known and thrill in what felt new.

"You missed me," he teased between kisses.

"I missed... this," she whispered.

Their connection was like a current, equal parts passion and healing. They moved together with a rhythm that had once been instinct and was now rediscovered.

Afterwards, they lay tangled beneath the sheets, the world finally blessedly still.

Naina traced lazy circles on Aryan's chest. "We can't ignore what's next. Board, the press, the backlash. The real battle would not be fought with guns or servers, but with reputations and relentless truths."

"I know," Aryan said. "But for once, I'm not doing it alone."

She looked up at him. "And I'm not running."

They didn't promise forever.

But in that moment, they didn't need to.

They had each other, and everything else could wait until morning.

***

Chapter 11

THE COLLAPSE OF SHADOWS

The apartment was dim, lit only by the glow of three laptop screens, and filled with the ambient thrum of server fans in the corner. The air smelled of burnt coffee and tension.

Aryan stood over the central table, his eyes scanning lines of metadata and financial trails. Naina typed furiously beside him, her screen littered with names of shell corporations, hidden transfers, and foreign tax havens.

"This one," she said, highlighting a string of transactions, "was funnelled from a fake educational NGO straight into a Seychelles-based trust. It links back to one of Vikram's shadow boards."

Aryan nodded. "It's not just a money trail. It's a human pipeline. They laundered identities the same way they laundered funds."

Anjali Kapoor, the head of public relations at TechNova, sat cross-legged on the rug, her phone tucked between her shoulder and ear. She ended a call and looked up. "My source at the cyber crimes division confirms," she said. "They've been building a case quietly, waiting for someone to pull the thread."

Aryan leaned on the table. "Well, we just pulled the whole spool."

As if on cue, Anjali's phone buzzed again. She opened the message, her eyes widening.

"Private server dump. Recovered emails. Vikram's signature. Direct orders to suppress data."

Naina whistled softly. "That's the smoking gun."

Aryan's jaw clenched. "Then we move now, before he finds a way to cover it, because monsters don't pause to rebuild walls once the first crack shatters them."

For a second, silence hung heavy in the room.

Then Aryan straightened. "We hit him where he's weakest, truth, delivered with precision. A scalpel, not a sledgehammer."

And in that moment, the plan began to crystallize, not just an operation, but a reckoning.

The wall-mounted monitor now displayed a countdown: 19 hours to Vikram Sharma's scheduled press conference.

Anjali pointed at the screen. "He's going to try and flip the narrative and paint himself as the misunderstood patriot," she said, her voice sharp. "He'll spin the investigation as political revenge."

Naina leaned back, arms crossed. "Then we don't fight him in the headlines; we rewrite them in real-time."

Aryan nodded slowly, his mind already racing. "We don't go on stage. We don't do a press meet. We let him stand under the lights… and then we collapse the floor beneath him."

He moved toward the whiteboard and drew a quick layout:

Anjali: coordinates with three independent media outlets to pre-load their stories for synchronized release.

Naina: prepares the data vault and tamper-proof timestamps on all files.

Aryan: oversees final intel vetting and coordinates with legal allies for immediate follow-up action.

"This is a digital ambush," Aryan said. "When he begins speaking, our evidence drops across encrypted channels, public media, and verified whistleblower networks."

Anjali smirked. "It's elegant. Surgical. Calculated chaos. Classic Mehra."

Naina added, "And untraceable. No public presence, no retaliation targets."

Aryan nodded. "If we do this right, we don't just expose Vikram, we end the illusion of control he's built around himself."

The plan wasn't just bold. It was personal. And they were ready.

Aryan's phone vibrated, no caller ID, no preview.

He tapped the message open.

Just five words, stark against a black background:

"You won't survive this storm."

No name. No trace. But Aryan knew. This was no bluff. It was Vikram's style, elegant menace with perfect timing.

He turned the screen to Naina and Anjali.

Anjali exhaled. "That's not desperation," she said. "That's confidence. He thinks he's still ahead."

Naina's jaw tightened. "He's scared. Otherwise he wouldn't need to rattle cages."

Aryan set the phone down slowly. "It doesn't change anything."

But Naina noticed the hesitation in his voice. His shoulders were too stiff, his fingers unmoving.

She stood up and moved close to him. "He's already lost control, Aryan," she said in a voice low enough for only him to hear. "You're the threat now, not the other way around."

Aryan met her eyes. The doubt still flickered behind his, but so did something else—resolve.

Anjali stood up as well, brushing dust off her jeans. "Take a break, both of you. I'll keep prepping the media channels."

Aryan hesitated, then nodded, stepping out onto the small balcony off the server room. Naina followed him.

The night air hit cool against their faces.

"I thought I could outplay people like him without becoming like him," Aryan murmured.

"You haven't," Naina said softly. "You're building light, not shadows."

Behind them, the screen still blinked: 18 hours remaining.

And the storm was just beginning. But this time, it would carry their thunder.

***

Aryan stood by the open window, his reflection showing in the glass. His hands hovered over his phone, uncertain for once.

He needed clarity. Not a strategy. Not another encrypted feed or legal opinion. Something quieter. Wiser.

And there was only one person who had ever helped him make sense of the world when it turned dark: Arvind Patel. Aryan had met him during his second year at Stanford, an ethics professor on sabbatical from IIM Ahmedabad. Arvind wasn't loud. He didn't believe in headlines. But his words had stayed with Aryan longer than any algorithm or corporate playbook.

He had once said, "If truth costs you everything but your soul, you're still ahead."

Aryan dialled his number.

The phone rang once. Then again.

And then: "Aryan?"

Aryan's chest eased just a little. "It's been a long time, sir," he said.

Arvind's voice was as steady as ever. "Too long. You sound like a man who's trying not to drown."

"I think I'm about to change the tide," Aryan replied. "But I need to know it's worth it."

"Is this revenge?" Arvind asked gently. "Or responsibility?"

Aryan looked down at the flashing news alerts on his tablet. "Responsibility."

"Then hold your ground," Arvind said. "You don't need to be loud. Just true."

Aryan closed his eyes. That's what he'd needed. No approval. Not reassurance. Just that one steady anchor.

"Thank you," he said softly.

"No," Arvind replied. "Thank you for still knowing where to call."

Aryan stepped back into the room, the burden in his eyes replaced by resolve.

Naina looked up from her screen. "Is everything okay?"

He gave a tight nod. "It is now. Let's finish this."

The air inside the safehouse buzzed with purpose. Anjali was on her third call in fifteen minutes, cross-checking upload times with two independent media outlets and a whistleblower site. "Confirming with *The Wire* and *Scroll*," she said. "Backup files sent to NetPulse in Singapore. All embargoed until we trigger."

Naina worked silently beside her, compiling the final data vault. "Encrypted, hashed, and time-stamped. Tamper logs initiated. Once we release, no one can question its authenticity."

Aryan moved to the whiteboard and made a final adjustment. "We stagger it; three waves, one every thirty seconds. Let the impact ripple."

Anjali tapped her pen. "What about timing?"

Aryan nodded at the monitor. "Vikram speaks at 8 p.m. We drop at 8:02, right as he hits his talking points."

Naina added, "Our servers are isolated. DDoS protections are active, so even if they try flooding us with fake traffic to crash the site, the mirror backups will auto-activate."

Anjali smirked. "It's like punching him in the face with facts."

Aryan looked at them, this team of fighters, thinkers, and believers.

It wasn't just about taking Vikram down anymore. It was about redefining what truth looked like in a world trained to ignore it.

***

Anjali's phone buzzed. She glanced at it and swore under her breath.

"He's moved the press conference. It's now at 6:30 p.m., not 8."

Naina looked up sharply. "That's 90 minutes from now."

Aryan stepped forward. "Why?" he asked, frowning.

Anjali tossed the phone onto the table. "He's scared. He wants to control the story before anything else breaks."

Naina stood up, already rerouting server protocols. "Then we don't wait for 8:02. We hit him on his entrance, not his applause."

Aryan nodded. "Reverse the sequence. The moment he starts, boom! Wave One goes live. Every site. Every outlet."

Anjali was already on the phone again. "I'll update all media partners, tell them to prepare their headlines and hold the trigger."

Aryan moved to the window. Outside, the sun had started to dip, casting long shadows across the city skyline. It was symbolic, almost poetic. The hour of reckoning had simply arrived early.

He turned back to the team. "A change of timing doesn't change the mission. It just makes it cleaner. The sooner he speaks, the sooner we strip away the performance."

Naina finished typing and hit 'Enter'. "Vault synchronized. Countdown adjusted. We're back on track."

Aryan exhaled. "Then we strike while he's still smiling."

The battle wouldn't wait for perfect timing. So, they would make the moment perfect instead.

The digital clock on Naina's laptop ticked down: 57 minutes to launch.

Aryan stood behind her, his arms crossed, as she verified the final passcodes. "Checksum verified. Vault sealed. Decryption is only possible once the key hits the broadcast feed."

Anjali spun her tablet toward them. "Journalists are in standby mode. Our drop signal will hit three major networks and twelve independent platforms in the first wave."

Aryan pointed at the second screen. "And the second wave?"

Naina answered without looking up, "Foreign press—Southeast Asia, European outlets, and diaspora-led feeds. They'll spread it beyond Vikram's reach. Even if local media gets suppressed, it'll be out of his hands in under two minutes."

Aryan paced the room once. "Good. No bottlenecks. No single point of failure."

Anjali smirked. "I trained with you, remember?"

He gave her a quick grin, then asked, "Communications check?"

Naina raised her hand. "Channel Alpha active. Audio only. No names, no identifiers."

Anjali adjusted her earpiece. "T-minus fifty-five."

They took their positions: Naina at the encryption console, Anjali at the media dispatch, Aryan at a central hub, monitoring system integrity.

There was silence now, not the silence of fear but of focus. No adrenaline. Just preparation.

The kind of stillness you feel before a wave crashes, when the ocean pulls back for just a moment, and you realize there's no going back.

Naina's system chimed. It was not a server alert, but a private message. Encrypted. Untraceable. Just like the others.

She opened it cautiously, her breath catching as she read the words:

"It won't be Aryan who pays. Watch the ones you love." She froze.

Aryan noticed her expression instantly. "What is it?" he asked.

Naina hesitated, then turned the screen toward him and Anjali. Aryan's jaw tightened as he read the warning. The colour drained slightly from his face from fear of what it meant.

"They're trying to break our timing," he muttered. "Distract us. Shake our hand just before we strike."

Anjali looked up. "Do we pull back?"

"No," replied Aryan, his voice steady. "We accelerate."

Naina's fingers hesitated above the keyboard. "But what if…"

Aryan stepped close and said in a low voice, "We can't afford to blink now. We've come too far. And we're not alone. We protect each other, just like always." Then he added, "We don't fight threats with fear. We answer them with light."

She stared at him, her mind in a whirl, then nodded.

Her hands moved again, faster now. Sharper. Like every keystroke mattered.

Anjali said, "Forty-five minutes."

Outside, the sky darkened.

Inside, the room glowed with purpose.

And the line between fear and fury had finally vanished.

***

The tension in the room was electric and raw, but held steady by the gravity of what they were about to unleash.

Aryan stood near the whiteboard, now covered with final arrows, time stamps, and fallback routes. He turned to face Naina and Anjali, his voice calm but steel-edged.

"This isn't about embarrassing him," he said. "It's not about headlines or being first."

Anjali nodded, folding her arms. "It's about impact."

Aryan pointed to the screen. "When this data drops, we're not just exposing corruption but also collapsing his web of his companies, his connections, his political armour, one thread at a time."

Naina leaned forward. "That's why he's lashing out now. He knows it's not just personal, it's structural."

Aryan looked at her, then at Anjali. "And it only works if we stay the course. No second-guessing. No glory chasing. We stay invisible and let the truth speak."

Anjali smirked. "That's a first for you."

Aryan grinned faintly. "Growth."

He turned serious again. "This is the moment," he said. "Vikram will step up to that podium, thinking he owns the room. But for the first time, he won't know the rules because we're writing them."

Silence fell, but it wasn't fear anymore. It was readiness. Naina glanced at the countdown: 00:31:12.

Aryan exhaled slowly. "From this point on," he said, "we don't look back."

***

The clock on the screen ticked down to 00:14:39.

The team moved with quiet urgency, each motion rehearsed, refined, resolved.

Anjali adjusted her headset and tapped into the encrypted media channel. "The outlets are ready," she said. "International nodes are synced. We'll cascade across eight zones in the first wave."

Naina ran a final system diagnostic test. "No drop in bandwidth," she said. "Vaults are primed. Emergency servers in Zurich and Tokyo are mirroring every fifteen seconds."

Aryan checked his tablet, red dots showing known network vulnerabilities, all blocked. "Encryption logs clean. No traces. Once we send this, we're ghosts."

Anjali looked up from her terminal. "And Vikram?"

Naina swivelled her screen. "Live feed confirms he's at the venue, stepping behind the curtain now. His speech will begin on time."

Aryan stood at the centre of the room, the hum of monitors around him like an orchestra waiting for its downbeat. "This is it," he said. "Final check. No hesitation. No retraction."

"Two minutes until stream intercept activates," Naina said, fingers hovering over the primary trigger key.

Anjali looked at Aryan. "I've alerted the clean press pool," she said. "The second this hits, they're pushing a unified headline."

Aryan nodded once, his gaze sweeping across both women. "Let's do this for the ones who never had a microphone. Who never got to speak."

The countdown blinked: 00:01:57

No alarms.

No panic.

Just execution.

***

The room was silent, except for the low hum of the live stream.

On the main monitor, Vikram Sharma stood behind a polished podium in an opulent conference hall. The press surged forward, cameras blinking, microphones thrust forward.

He adjusted his tie, smiled, and began: "Good evening. Thank you all for being here."

Naina glanced at Aryan.

He gave a single nod.

She tapped the trigger key.

Instantly, a series of green lights rippled across the status board. One by one, the payloads launched: emails, financial records, trafficking files, confidential memos, all wrapped in bulletproof verification seals.

Anjali's phone buzzed.

"First outlet confirmed," she said. "Now it's spreading."

Within seconds, there was another alert. "Singapore feed picked it up," confirmed Anjali.

Naina's screen glowed as distribution nodes flared to life. "Tokyo. London. Zurich. Backdoors holding," she said, eyes glued to the screen.

Aryan turned back to the livestream.

Vikram was still talking, completely unaware.

Then it started.

A flurry of murmurs.

Journalists looking at their phones.

A few glanced at each other. One stepped back and whispered into a producer's ear.

Vikram faltered mid-sentence.

He looked down, then back up, his eyes just barely twitching.

Aryan folded his arms. "He feels it."

Anjali muttered, "He just doesn't know what hit him yet."

Naina leaned back, eyes calm. "But he will."

Onscreen, Vikram stammered.

And then the collapse began.

Not with explosions, but with truth breaking every carefully built lie.

On the livestream, the shift was unmistakable.

Vikram's voice faltered again. Then, he stopped speaking altogether.

Behind the cameras, chaos spread like a virus.

Phones buzzed. Tablets lit up. Reporters who had arrived ready to nod along now glanced at each other with sudden urgency.

"*The Wire* just pushed the story. 'Vikram's Shell Empire: The Files Behind the Fall.' It's everywhere," Anjali reported.

Aryan stepped closer to the screen. "He knows now."

Naina added, "Every drop validated. Every signature is traceable. He is about to be the face of everything he buried."

On screen, Vikram blinked rapidly and motioned to someone offstage. His aide rushed forward and whispered something into his ear. Vikram's confident posture had dissolved into panic cloaked in denial.

Then came the questions.

Loud. Relentless.

"Mr Sharma, are these documents authentic?"

"Do you deny involvement with the trafficking network?"

"Why did you suppress evidence tied to Mediscan protocols?"

Vikram stepped back, shook his head, but said nothing.

No statement.

No plan.

No script.

Just raw exposure.

Anjali leaned forward. "Watch him," she said. "He's trying to decide whether to run or lie."

Naina didn't blink. "Either way, we win."

The screen froze for a moment as the broadcast tried to recalibrate.

But the world had already seen it. No edit button could undo the moment. And as Vikram stumbled away from the stage, truth had already taken his place.

***

Chapter 12

DAYLIGHT RECKONING

The silence after the collapse was heavier than the fall itself.

For a moment, no one moved. No cameras flashed. No questions were shouted out.

There was just the weight of the truth, undeniable and raw, engulfing the room like a slow avalanche. The first real sound was the low, urgent murmur of the reporters.

Then came the flickers.

Phones lifted. Screens glowed. Journalists huddled together, exchanging frantic whispers and fact-checks. Already, live broadcasts were cutting away, not to censorship, but to panels dissecting the bombshell leaks Aryan's team had unleashed.

Vikram Sharma stood behind the podium, gripping its edges, trying to gather words that had already abandoned him. His notes lay forgotten. His planned speech was irrelevant now. He tried to speak, tried to reclaim the floor. But every word he started died against the rising tide of real-time scandal. A camera caught him wiping sweat from his brow. Another zoomed in on the frantic hand signals of his aides by the curtain, pleading, planning, failing.

Aryan, Naina, and Anjali watched remotely.

The truth had already spoken louder than any accusation.

And now, it was no longer a press conference. It was an unravelling. The man who had once towered over boardrooms and ministers now looked unbearably small.

It was a public, irreversible disintegration of a man who once thought he was invincible.

***

The floodgates opened.

"Mr Vikram, are you aware your NGO was used to launder offshore assets?"

"Is it true you ordered the deletion of internal QA reports on Mediscan's AI failures?"

"What do you say about the verified documents circulating right now with your personal signature?"

Vikram blinked under the barrage of questions. The lights felt hotter. His throat tightened, but he forced a practised smile.

"I am not here to respond to fabricated narratives from hostile actors."

But his voice cracked, betraying the calm mask he tried to wear.

Another voice shouted, "So the screenshots are fake? The financial records? The biometric databases?"

Vikram's response was a beat too slow.

A second reporter stood up. "Can you deny you attended a board meeting in Singapore listed under one of your proxy shell companies?" he asked.

Vikram's aide approached with a tablet in hand, whispering frantically. Vikram ignored it. The walls of confidence he'd so carefully erected were now mirrors, each question reflecting a truth he could no longer dodge.

The cameras zoomed in on him.

He adjusted his tie. He tried to speak, but words failed him. From the back of the room, someone livestreamed the entire moment to a million viewers. In the comment feed, hashtags surged:

#VikramExposed

#MinistryOfSilence

#MediscanFiles

Vikram looked down at his notes.

They no longer mattered.

Because the room had already made its decision.

***

The room was already splintering under pressure when the double doors at the back of the hall opened quietly, without fanfare.

Heads turned.

And then, everything stopped.

Aryan Mehra and Naina Rao walked down the aisle, side by side. No microphones. No bodyguards. Just intent.

Vikram saw them. For a split second, his polished mask cracked. The timing was brutal, seconds after the data had detonated online, minutes after the press had turned.

The architects of the collapse now stood in front of him.

Vikram blinked once, as if hoping they were an illusion he could wish away.

Aryan didn't speak at first. He didn't have to.

The media buzz quietened down. All lenses shifted.

Vikram tried to recover himself. "Well, well... If it isn't the fugitives of public fiction. Are you here to gloat?"

Naina's voice cut through the air, clear, unshaken. "No. We're here to make sure you don't rewrite the ending."

A ripple passed through the room.

Aryan took a step forward. "You played your part, Sharma," he said. "You sold silence for power. You buried lives behind data and profit. But now, your firewall is gone."

Vikram's lips curled. "Do you think walking in here makes you a hero?" he sneered.

"No," Aryan replied. "Just the consequence you didn't see coming."

He turned slightly to the cameras, the press, the world watching.

"This isn't revenge," Aryan said. "This is daylight."

Vikram squared his shoulders, forcing a chuckle that didn't quite reach his eyes. "I see you've embraced your flair for drama, Aryan. What's next, flash drives as party favours?"

The journalists didn't laugh.

Neither did Aryan.

Naina took the microphone from the front podium. She didn't need permission to do so.

"This isn't theatre," she said. "It's testimony. You wrote this tragedy, Vikram. We're just reading it aloud."

She turned to the crowd. "The financial trails. The shell corporations. The AI-driven medical filters that profile people by class and caste. It's all verified. And it's live."

Screens in the half still connected to media feeds flashed headlines in real-time:

"Exclusive: Vikram Sharma's Mediscan Empire Funded via Offshore Trusts."

"Whistleblower Leak Links Sharma to Trafficking Cover-Up."

Vikram stepped forward. "This is a smear campaign," he said, his voice rising. "There's no context, no proof these documents aren't manipulated."

Aryan met his gaze. "The proof is time-stamped, cross-referenced, and blockchain-verified. You can shout, but the servers won't care."

Someone in the press gallery stood up. "Vikram Sharma, do you deny meeting with tech intermediaries flagged in the Singapore data logs?"

Another question. Another angle. Another strike.

Naina looked at Vikram, her voice quieter now. "You used people like numbers," she accused. "Like margins on a spreadsheet. But people remember."

Vikram's voice cracked. "You think you're clean? You ran, Aryan. You hid."

Aryan took a deep breath. "I didn't hide. I rebuilt. And now I'm here," he said in a steady voice.

The last of Vikram's bravado drained from his face, leaving only a man cornered by his own greed.

And Vikram, for the first time, had nothing left to say. The room didn't erupt. It fell silent.

But the silence didn't last long. A low murmur swept through the audience, like wind through dry grass before a blaze. Reporters looked at each other, their expressions a mix of disbelief and excitement.

Then, one by one, phones were lifted. Camera shutters clicked. Recordings resumed. Live tweets, voice notes, and whispered updates to editors began. "Are you getting this?"

"Push it now."

"This is bigger than we thought."

At the rear, a young journalist whispered to her colleague, "They walked in like scalpel cuts. No flash. Just facts."

Vikram saw it. All of it.

And it was worse than yelling. Worse than a protest. It was incredulity wrapped in quiet condemnation.

Someone stood up in the second row and walked out, not out of protest, but certainty. He had heard enough.

Aryan and Naina didn't move. They didn't need to. They had already said everything that mattered.

Vikram scanned the crowd, searching for allies. He found none.

The podium in front of him felt hostile. The cameras weren't his anymore; they belonged to the truth now.

He looked like a man still trying to remember his lines after the play had ended.

"You made people disappear in the shadows," Naina said, her voice breaking into his trepidation. "All we did was turn on the light."

More people stood up, not in applause or in protest.

They were just done listening. Done believing.

The silence in the room had shifted. It wasn't passive anymore; it was judgemental. Every face in the room seemed to ask the same unspoken question:

What now?

Vikram's voice, when it came, was brittle. "You want a villain?" he asked. "Fine. Paint me as one. But don't pretend this circus is about justice. It's revenge. Nothing more."

Aryan didn't flinch. "It was never about revenge."

Vikram sneered. "Spoken like a man who hid behind servers and surrogate statements."

Anjali's voice rang from the side of the hall, where she'd been streaming the entire confrontation live. "Except this time, the servers spoke back. With receipts."

A ripple of amusement and affirmation moved through the audience.

Vikram turned, pointing at Naina. "She fabricated half of it," he accused. "A disgruntled data analyst-turned-cyber vigilante!"

"Then disprove it," said Naina, unperturbed. "The files are public. The timestamps are real. The signatures are yours."

More eyes turned to Vikram.

He stepped back from the podium, waving to his aide. "We're done here."

But even that command fell flat.

Security hesitated.

Cameras zoomed in.

A prominent anchor near the front spoke into her microphone: "We're witnessing the dismantling of a narrative that held power for far too long."

Vikram looked directly at Aryan one last time.

There was no rage left. Just fear. And in a room he once ruled, Vikram now stood completely alone.

***

Two floors above the conference hall, in a discreet operations room, a wall of monitors displayed the unfolding chaos below.

One screen showed Vikram Sharma retreating from the podium. Another showed a live dashboard of leaked documents, downloaded thousands of times in the last 30 minutes. DCP Rajesh Kumar stood in the centre, headset in place, his expression like granite.

"Do we have full verification?" he asked.

The cybercrime officer beside him nodded. "Every signature matches," he said. "Financial trails trace clean. The whistleblower authentication key just pinged back from three countries."

Rajesh didn't hesitate. "Send the report. Notify the DCP and request a judicial seal. Warrants are cleared. He doesn't leave that building."

Another officer picked up the intercom and said, "Team Delta, move to intercept. Stage exit. Block all vehicle access routes. No alarms, just containment."

Downstairs, Vikram whispered urgently to his security aide, "Call the car. Now."

The aide nodded, but hesitated, eyes drifting to the press, to the silent uniformed officers moving subtly into position along the side walls.

Something had shifted. Vikram wasn't an untouchable anymore.

On Anjali's livestream, a notification pinged:

"Sources confirm legal motion issued against Vikram Sharma. Assets under freeze review."

In the background of the frame, a figure moved near the security perimeter. Calm. Controlled.

It was Commandant Avaneesh Kumar, flanked by two plainclothes officers.

No sirens.

No shouts.

Just the quiet inevitability of accountability.

***

The room was dim, the glow of multiple screens casting sharp shadows across the bare walls. Aryan set his jaw, eyes locked onto the live feed streaming Vikram's collapsing press conference.

Journalists surged forward, shouting over each other.

"Mr Sharma, is it true your logistics company was used for trafficking?"

"Do you deny authorizing the Nova shipments?"

Vikram floundered, his polished mask slipping. Sweat gleamed on his forehead under the brutal attack.

Aryan tapped the screen, pausing the chaos. "He's losing control," he said. "Now we press harder."

Naina leaned in, her voice low and sharp. "Rajesh's units have positioned themselves at all major exit routes. Kabir's intercepting traffic cameras. Vikram's cornered, he just doesn't know it yet."

Kabir's voice crackled through the earpiece, irreverent as ever:

"Cornered rats are the worst, bossman. Expect dirty tricks."

Aryan's eyes narrowed. "Let him try."

Across the table, Anjali refreshed an encrypted feed from TechNova's internal servers. "Financial flags raised. The shell accounts are frozen. His corporate lifelines are dead," she reported.

Aryan's hand closed around his coffee mug. "Perfect. Cut the money. Cut the escape."

Naina tapped rapidly on her tablet, sending one final batch of evidence to trusted news outlets. "The media will flood with the real story by morning. He won't survive the headlines."

Aryan's voice was razor-edged. "We're not waiting for morning."

He stood up, putting on his jacket with deliberate calm.

"Tonight, we end Vikram Sharma's empire," he said quietly.

Naina rose silently beside him. The final hunt was about to begin.

***

Kabir's voice snapped in Aryan's ear as they exited the safehouse.

"Alert. Vikram just abandoned the podium. Moving fast. Looks panicked."

Aryan and Naina exchanged a grim look.

"Which direction?" Aryan barked, already weaving through the crowded street toward their car.

"North exit, Vidyapeetha side," Kabir confirmed. "He's ditched his security detail. It looks like he's aiming for a secondary escape route."

Aryan threw himself into the driver's seat, and the engine roared to life.

"He knows the net is closing," Naina said, her voice tight. "This isn't a controlled retreat. He's desperate. Desperation wasn't part of his plan."

Kabir's laugh crackled over the line. "Desperate men make sloppy mistakes. I'm opening real-time satellite eyes, giving you a clean tail."

Aryan steered into traffic, cutting through late-night commuters with surgical precision. "Are Rajesh's teams in position?" he asked.

"Affirmative," Kabir said. "Perimeter is closing from three sides. There's only a slim chance he breaks through, and that's if he's stupidly lucky."

Naina's fingers danced across her tablet, pulling up Vikram's known safehouses, financial withdrawals, and burner phone trails.

"He has fallback options," she muttered. "Hidden exits he never listed officially. We need to outthink him, not just outgun him."

Aryan's voice was icy. "We will."

The city blurred around them, neon lights, autorickshaws, security barricades flickering past.

Ahead, Bangalore's arteries throbbed with life.

But for Vikram Sharma, every path was narrowing into a noose.

And this time, there would be no escape plan clever enough to save him.

The darkened streets flashed past as Aryan swerved onto a service lane, headlights cutting through misty patches.

Kabir's voice buzzed again.

"New intel: Vikram's personal driver picked up a sealed package fifteen minutes ago. Could be cash, fake IDs, maybe even a clean passport. He's preparing for a full burn."

Naina leaned forward, tension coiling in her muscles. "It means he's not just running. He's disappearing."

Aryan's grip tightened on the wheel. "Not tonight," he said grimly.

"We've intercepted chatter from one of his logistics moles," Anjali's voice cut in from the backup unit. "Codeword 'Black Kite' confirmed. His emergency exit plan is active."

"Black Kite?" Aryan repeated, a grim smile twisting his mouth. "So he does have friends left, some shadowy ones."

"Council type friends?" Naina asked sharply.

Aryan shook his head. "Maybe. But let's not waste time chasing phantoms tonight."

Naina nodded. "Let's focus on the rat we can catch."

Their communication units buzzed again. It was DCP Rajesh this time, his voice crisp and direct.

"Units in place. Target sighted heading toward the old market district. He's on foot now."

Aryan's heart kicked into a sprint.

"He's cornered," Naina said, already pulling up street layouts. "But he'll fight like hell."

Aryan's jaw was set. "Then we fight smarter."

The black sedan roared down a narrow lane, every second slicing away Vikram's chances.

In the chessboard of the city, the king was trapped.

And checkmate was seconds away.

***

Chapter 13

THE CHASE - NO MERCY LEFT

Aryan sat behind the wheel of the unmarked sedan, engine idling, his knuckles drumming an impatient rhythm on the steering wheel. Beside him, Naina flipped through traffic surveillance grids on her tablet, her brow furrowed.

"Vikram's slippery as hell," Aryan muttered, eyes scanning the empty street ahead. "If he clears the city perimeter, we'll be chasing ghosts."

"He's aiming for the old city centre," Naina said crisply, stabbing a finger at the map. "Narrow alleys, local traffic…a nightmare to navigate. Perfect for disappearing."

Aryan smirked, a glint in his eyes. "Ah, where even thoughts have to stand in line to move."

"Focus," Naina snapped, though the corner of her mouth twitched. "Rajesh's team's setting up blockades. We still have a chance to box him in."

"Assuming he doesn't have another ace up his sleeve," Aryan said, shifting gears. "Or another mole in the system."

Their eyes met, a silent understanding flashing between them; failure was not an option. Neither of them dared admit it aloud, but the cost of failure tonight was personal, too personal.

Aryan tapped his earpiece. "Kabir, status?"

Kabir's voice crackled to life, full of irreverent cheer. "Your rat just passed Camera Grid 7B, heading east. I'm clearing a path. Green lights for you all the way, bossman."

Naina shot Aryan a glance. "Let's move."

Aryan floored the accelerator.

Every heartbeat matched the thrum of the engine.

Tonight wasn't about winning. It was about survival. And catching a man who had no intention of going quietly.

The streets of Bangalore opened up before them. Aryan wove the sedan through late-night traffic with ruthless precision. Cars, motorbikes, autorickshaws, and lumbering buses clogged the roadways, each vehicle another obstacle between them and their quarry.

Naina gripped the dashboard, her voice sharp. "Left! He's cutting across towards KR Market."

Aryan didn't hesitate. Tyres squealed as he swung the car around, narrowly missing a vendor cart piled high with mangoes. Horns blared in protest, but Aryan's focus was absolute.

"He's desperate," Naina said, eyes scanning ahead. "No plan, just running."

"Cornered rats bite the hardest," Aryan muttered, glancing at the glowing dot on his GPS tracker, Vikram's last known ping.

In his earpiece, Kabir's voice chimed in, cool and steady. "Traffic's a nightmare up ahead. Diverting you through Commercial Street. You'll gain a block on him."

"Good," Aryan snapped. "Keep clearing."

As they barrelled forward, Aryan caught a glimpse of flashing blue lights a few streets over. Rajesh's units were setting up roadblocks.

"We're squeezing him," Naina said, her tone edged with steel.

Aryan nodded grimly. "Now we just have to make sure he doesn't squeeze through."

The city roared around them, the wail of sirens, the metallic cacophony of a metropolis that never truly slept. Every turn, every flash of movement could be Vikram, or another dead end.

But Aryan and Naina didn't falter.

Tonight, the city was a battlefield.

And they were the hunters.

"Kabir, we need you to pull a rabbit out of the hat. Now," Aryan barked into his earpiece, swerving past a slow-moving bus with inches to spare.

Kabir's unruffled voice crackled through, tinged with humour. "Relax, bossman. Bangalore's traffic grid is my playground."

Naina kept her eyes glued to the screen, tracking Vikram's moving blip. "He's three blocks ahead, cutting through Commercial Street. If he hits the flyover, we'll lose him."

"Not happening," Kabir said. "Hold tight."

A few furious keystrokes echoed over the line, and suddenly, traffic lights ahead blinked in rapid succession. Red turned green. Cross-street traffic stalled. Pedestrians scrambled back to the sidewalks.

Aryan grinned. "Remind me to give you a raise."

"I accept cash, crypto, and lifetime supplies of *biryani*," Kabir quipped.

Naina cut in sharply. "Less jokes, more magic, Kabir."

"Already waving my wand, bosslady," he replied. "Clearing next three intersections. Vikram's boxed in unless he grows wings."

The car surged forward, every turn clearing just as they approached. Vikram's silver sedan flickered into view, momentarily trapped behind a delivery truck.

"There!" Aryan shouted, slamming the gear down. The sedan's tyres screamed in protest, but momentum was on their side.

Naina's pulse pounded in her ears, but her voice stayed cool. "Keep tight. Don't spook him yet."

Aryan nodded grimly. "Let the rat think he's winning."

The path ahead stayed open, just enough for Aryan and Naina to keep chasing Vikram.

***

The sedan skidded around a corner, and suddenly, they were swallowed by the chaos of the old market district.

Colours exploded around them: sari stalls full of vibrant silks, spices piled high in mounds, flower garlands swinging from makeshift stands. The air was thick with the heady scents of jasmine, diesel, and frying *samosas*.

Aryan cursed under his breath. "Perfect," he said. "He's diving into the one place CCTV dreams go to die."

"Stay on him!" Naina snapped, already popping open her door before the car fully stopped.

Aryan jerked the handbrake, sending the sedan into a controlled skid between two abandoned fruit carts. In one fluid motion, they were both out and running, weaving through the dense, noisy crowd.

"Visual on Vikram, two o'clock!" Naina shouted, eyes locking onto the flash of a silver-grey suit pushing through the throng.

Kabir's voice crackled in their earpieces. "Warning: you're flying blind in there. No camera coverage. You're on your own."

"Thanks for the pep talk!" Aryan grunted, dodging a wiry man balancing a stack of papayas.

Vikram moved fast, slipping through a spice stall and nearly upending a crate of turmeric. Vendors cursed and grabbed at him, momentarily slowing him down.

Aryan and Naina seized the advantage, cutting the distance.

Every second counted now. The crowd, the noise, the smells, all blurred into a wall of sensory overload. Only Vikram's retreating figure remained sharply defined.

"Don't lose him!" Naina barked, her voice cutting through the din like a whip.

"Wasn't planning to," Aryan shot back, teeth bared in a fierce grin.

In this living, breathing chaos, the real chase had just begun.

Aryan's heart hammered against his ribs as he vaulted over a fallen crate, landing in a crouch. Through the swirl of colour and chaos, he spotted a flash of silver disappearing behind a row of vegetable stalls.

"There!" he barked, pointing sharply.

Naina didn't hesitate. She bolted ahead, cutting through the crowd with a precision that Aryan could only admire.

They broke free from the market's tight alleys and stumbled into a side lane where Vikram's getaway car, a dusty silver sedan, roared to life.

"He's trying to bolt!" Naina shouted.

Aryan's adrenaline surged. "Back to the car, now!"

They sprinted, shoes hammering against the cracked pavement. The black sedan waited like a loyal steed, battered but unbroken.

Aryan threw himself behind the wheel, slamming the door shut as Naina dove into the passenger seat. Tyres screeched as he floored the accelerator, the car fishtailing before surging forward.

Vikram's tail lights flickered ahead, weaving through handcarts and startled pedestrians.

"Shortcut ahead!" Naina said, scanning the navigation on her tablet. "Left, then sharp right onto Brigade Road. We can cut him off!"

Aryan swerved the wheel hard, ignoring the protests of physics as they barrelled through a side street barely wider than the car itself.

In the distance, Vikram's sedan wove dangerously through oncoming traffic, but Aryan was gaining on him, each second closing the gap.

"This ends tonight," Aryan muttered, his jaw tight.

Naina's eyes glinted with the same fierce resolve. "No matter what."

It was a wild, thundering chase in the heavy Bangalore night.

And neither side intended to surrender.

Vikram's sedan veered sharply off the main road, plunging into the gleaming sprawl of the tech district.

Aryan and Naina followed without hesitation, the black sedan roaring past glass-fronted skyscrapers and manicured corporate lawns. The change in scenery was drastic, from chaotic market streets to polished steel and neon reflections.

"He's trying to vanish into the corporate jungle, blend into the suits and security," Naina said, scanning the sterile, mirror-like facades.

Aryan's hands tightened on the wheel. "Not happening."

Ahead, Vikram's car jerked to a halt. The door flung open, and Vikram, shedding his jacket to look less conspicuous, darted into the swarm of office workers pouring out from a late-shift changeover.

"Ditching the car. Smart," Aryan growled.

Naina was already moving, throwing open her door before the sedan fully stopped. "On foot again!"

They slipped into the mass of bodies, blending seamlessly with the crowd, Aryan's blazer and Naina's dark jeans making them just another pair of stressed corporate warriors.

"He's heading toward Tower C," Kabir's voice chimed into their earpieces. "Security cam just pinged him. Level One lobby."

Aryan's eyes scanned the tide of workers, looking for a flash of messy hair, a too-expensive watch, a wrong kind of desperation.

"There!" Naina hissed, spotting Vikram sliding toward an elevator bank.

They quickened their pace, weaving through groups of laughing interns and bored security guards.

"He thinks he can lose us in here," Aryan said under his breath.

"Then let's remind him," Naina replied, her mouth set in a grim line, "that we wrote the book on surviving this city."

Above them, the high-rise towers blinked under the night sky… silent witnesses to the hunt that was underway.

***

Aryan pushed through the lobby doors, Naina right behind him. Vikram was already slipping past a security checkpoint, flashing a fake ID at the unsuspecting guards.

"He's trying to get to the underground parking!" Naina hissed.

Aryan tapped his earpiece. "Kabir, we're losing him. Cut the exits. Now."

Kabir's voice answered immediately, laced with excitement. "Already on it. Rerouting security protocols. Disabling parking shutters... now."

A moment later, a low mechanical whine echoed through the building. Steel gates began to descend over the basement exits, trapping cars inside.

"He's boxed in!" Naina said, sprinting ahead.

Vikram skidded to a halt, seeing the shutters slam down. He bolted sideways, heading for the pedestrian exit instead.

Aryan and Naina gave chase, their footsteps pounding across marble floors slick with humidity. Office workers scattered, startled cries in their wake. Shoes skidded. Coffee cups smashed against marble.

Kabir's voice crackled again. "Heads up, green light sequence activated outside Tower C. If he tries to make it to Brigade Road, you'll have clear lanes."

"Good," Aryan grunted. "We're cutting this off now."

Vikram burst into the open air, his breath coming in ragged gasps. He tried flagging a passing auto-rickshaw, but the driver, seeing the chaos behind him, sped away.

Vikram didn't waste a second. He spotted a delivery van left idling by the kerb, the driver nowhere in sight. Wrenching the door open, he threw himself inside and slammed the gear into drive. The van jerked forward, scraping a bollard as he sped away toward Brigade Road. Aryan and Naina were gaining on Vikram, every step fuelled by adrenaline and the relentless drumbeat of pursuit.

"This time," Aryan muttered, "no more running."

The neon skyline flashed overhead, the city's heartbeat pulsing in sync with the chase, unstoppable, inevitable.

Vikram's world was closing in.

And Aryan and Naina were the ones tightening the noose.

Vikram drove down the street, weaving through traffic like a hunted animal. Ahead, the entrance to Lalbagh Botanical Garden loomed, sprawling gates thrown open to the humid night.

"He's heading into Lalbagh!" Naina shouted, sprinting harder.

Aryan cursed under his breath but didn't slow. "Perfect. Trees, shadows, and a thousand places to hide."

The moment they crossed the gate, the atmosphere changed. The bright lights of the city gave way to deep, verdant darkness. Banyan trees stretched their limbs across winding paths. The air was cooler, damp with the scent of soil and crushed leaves.

"Stay sharp," Naina warned, her breathing ragged.

Their footsteps muffled against the packed earth trails, Aryan scanned the paths ahead. In the moonlight and the glow from scattered garden lamps, Vikram's figure flickered like a ghost among the trees.

"He's trying to lose us in the foliage," Aryan growled.

"Not happening," Naina replied, quickening her pace.

Kabir's voice crackled faintly in their earpieces. "No drone coverage inside the garden. You're on your own. Play nice, kids."

Aryan smirked grimly. "We'll manage."

They darted past a water lily pond, the glassy surface rippling with the slight breeze. Statues and flowerbeds blurred past as they pushed deeper into the labyrinthine pathways.

There was a flash of movement ahead: Vikram, shoving through a hedge line, desperate to disappear.

"There!" Aryan shouted, veering left.

The garden seemed to conspire with Vikram, every twist and shadow offering a new escape. But Aryan and Naina moved with relentless precision, hunters tracking wounded prey.

Every step was a promise.

Every heartbeat, a countdown.

And Vikram was running out of road.

***

The mud churned under their feet as Aryan and Naina sprinted deeper into Lalbagh's dense foliage.

Moonlight filtered through thick canopies, casting twisted shadows across the narrow paths. Every breath they drew was filled with the scent of damp earth, crushed grass, and something electric, the proximity of their prey.

"There!" Naina shouted, pointing through a break in the thicket.

Half-hidden behind an overgrown hedge, a delivery van sat abandoned, its front bumper wedged awkwardly against a clump of flowering shrubs. The driver's door stood open, the engine ticking faintly in the heavy night air.

"He ditched it inside the garden," Aryan panted, skidding to a stop beside the vehicle. "Smart move, blends into the chaos."

Naina's sharp gaze followed broken branches and trampled undergrowth leading away from the car. "Trail's fresh. He's running blind now."

Aryan nodded grimly. "No more vehicles. No backup. Just him and us."

Without wasting another second, they plunged forward, navigating the winding trails that twisted through groves of bamboo and ancient trees.

The city's noise faded behind them, replaced by the chirping of crickets and the heavy beat of their own footsteps.

Somewhere ahead, Vikram was stumbling through the labyrinth, desperate and disoriented.

"We're closing the gap," Aryan muttered, adrenaline sharpening his senses.

"Stay tight," Naina panted. "He's wounded, but cornered animals are the most dangerous."

Through the thick foliage, fleeting glimpses of movement teased them onward—a flash of a white shirt, the crunch of a misstep on dry leaves.

The hunt had entered its final phase.

And this time, there would be no escape.

"He's trying to double back!" Naina called out, voice sharp as a knife's edge.

Aryan barely caught a glimpse of Vikram slipping through a narrow side trail, dodging between a cluster of low-hanging banyan roots.

"Smart," Aryan said, changing direction instantly. "But not smart enough."

Naina surged ahead, her mind racing faster than her feet. She closed her eyes for a second, visualizing the garden's map, every pond, every hidden footpath.

"He's aiming for the southeast service gate," she said, eyes snapping open. "Shortcut through the orchid enclosure!"

Aryan trusted her instinct without question. He veered off the main trail, following Naina's lead through dense undergrowth.

The garden twisted around them, bursts of flowering orchids, stone benches slick with dew, narrow bridges arching over dry streambeds. It was beautiful, and it was a battlefield.

Ahead, Vikram crashed through a hedge, panic overriding caution.

"He's slowing down," Aryan observed, breathing hard. "He's losing steam."

"Good," Naina replied, voice flat. "Because I'm not."

They pushed harder. Naina took a sharp right, leading Aryan onto a hidden shortcut between two massive flowering groves.

Suddenly, Vikram stumbled into view again, disoriented, trapped between the garden's labyrinth and his pursuers.

Aryan grinned through gritted teeth. "Got you!"

Vikram looked back once, and the terror in his eyes was unmistakable.

"No more escape routes," Naina said quietly, her words almost lost to the night breeze.

The hunt was almost over.

And for Vikram, the beautiful garden had become a cage.

***

Vikram glanced back, saw Aryan's outstretched hand just metres away, and made a desperate gamble.

He lunged sideways, crashing through a thin patch of undergrowth, thorns tearing at his arms. For one frantic moment, he vanished into the foliage.

Aryan cursed, adjusting course. Naina sprinted after him without hesitation.

The dense garden abruptly gave way, and Vikram, breathless and wild-eyed, stumbled out onto the wide lawns beyond Lalbagh's fence. The illuminated dome of the Vidhana Soudha towered ahead like a stone sentinel.

"There!" Naina shouted, pointing.

"He's running on fumes," Aryan said grimly. "But he's still dangerous."

Vikram, sensing the tightening noose, made a reckless decision. He plunged into a small crowd gathered near the monument's front steps, tourists and late-shift workers lingering for photos.

Before anyone could react, Vikram yanked a small knife from beneath his shirt, a thin, vicious-looking blade, and seized a young woman from behind.

The woman screamed. The crowd gasped.

Aryan's gut twisted. They were seconds away from tragedy.

"Stay back!" Vikram bellowed, pressing the blade's edge against the woman's throat. His hands trembled, the knife catching the floodlight's glare.

Aryan and Naina froze mid-run, instantly raising their hands.

"Vikram, listen!" Aryan's voice cut the thick night air. "This isn't the way out."

Vikram's chest heaved, the knife twitching dangerously close to the hostage's throat. The woman whimpered, terror etched across her face.

Police sirens screamed closer, blue and red lights splashing across the great stone facade behind them.

In Aryan's earpiece, Kabir whispered urgently, "Commandant's team is thirty seconds out. Stall him, Aryan. Stall him!"

Naina shifted subtly, circling half a step to the left, splitting Vikram's frantic focus.

"You're not a killer, Vikram," she said evenly. "You never were. You don't have the stomach for it."

Vikram's eyes darted wildly between them, between freedom and a future in chains.

The endgame had begun.

The sirens grew louder.

From the street, Commandant Avaneesh Kumar's voice boomed through a loudspeaker, sharp and commanding. "Vikram Sharma, drop the weapon. You are surrounded. There's nowhere left to run."

Vikram flinched. Sweat dripped into his eyes. His hand shook visibly, the knuckles bloodless around the knife now pressed tighter against the hostage's trembling neck.

Aryan's voice stayed calm, anchored against the chaos. "Vikram, think. You pull that knife, you die right here. No second chances."

Naina edged a fraction closer, reading the tremor in Vikram's grip. "He's breaking," she whispered into her communication unit.

Vikram's breath came in ragged gasps. His gaze darted at Aryan, at Naina, at the advancing police lines, now barely twenty metres away.

"Let her go," Aryan urged, his voice low and deadly serious. "There's a way out. But not with blood on your hands."

For a moment, Vikram hesitated, and that was all Naina needed.

In one blur of motion, she pulled the compact taser from her belt and fired.

The electrodes punched into Vikram's side. Electricity jolted through his body. The knife clattered to the ground.

The hostage screamed and stumbled free, grabbed instantly by a nearby officer.

Vikram collapsed, muscles seizing, a strangled cry escaping his lips. Commandos swarmed in, securing him with swift, brutal precision.

Aryan exhaled, a deep, tired breath, as the adrenaline bled from his veins.

Naina moved to stand beside him, sweat trickling down her temples, but her eyes never leaving the chaos.

"Is it finally over?" she asked quietly.

Aryan watched as Vikram, now handcuffed and broken, was shoved into the waiting police van.

"No," Aryan said, his voice a dark promise. "Vikram was only the gatekeeper. The real architects are still out there."

Naina's expression hardened. "Then we hunt them next," she said grimly.

The sirens wailed into the thick night, but Aryan and Naina heard only the thrum of unfinished wars.

They stood together, battered but unyielding, ready for the battle still to come.

***

Chapter 14

THE END OF THE FALSE KING

The police convoy rumbled through the narrow streets, with Vikram shackled and slumped in the rear of the armoured van, flanked by two armed commandos.

Halfway to the holding facility, Vikram's body convulsed violently.

He gasped, clutching his chest, eyes rolling back.

"Medical emergency!" one of the commandos shouted.

The van screeched to a halt. Officers scrambled, radios crackling as they called for immediate diversion to the nearest hospital.

Minutes later, Vikram was wheeled into a sterile emergency room, guards flanking him tightly.

Doctors and nurses swarmed around him, but some faces were unfamiliar, too calm, too rehearsed.

One of the nurses, young, sharp-eyed, adjusted Vikram's IV line and leaned close.

In a whisper only he could hear, she said, "When the lights flicker, move left. Corridor B."

Vikram didn't react, but inside, adrenaline surged.

Seconds later, the hospital's power stuttered; just a flicker, barely enough to trigger an alarm.

Vikram sprang.

Aryan's instincts screamed from miles away. Something was wrong. It was too fast, too easy.

A scalpel was slipped into Vikram's hand.

There was a quick feint, a grunt, a flash of motion.

The nearest guard staggered, clutching his neck.

Vikram bolted down Corridor B, disappearing into the maze of emergency exits.

By the time full lockdown protocols were engaged, he was gone, swallowed up by the night, bleeding, half-dressed, but free.

Across the city, in the crumbling skeleton of half-built apartments, a safehouse light blinked twice, then once.

It was waiting.

And so was Vikram Sharma, broken, cornered, but not yet finished.

Once inside, Vikram paced like a caged animal. His fine suit was torn at the sleeves, his face streaked with grime and panic.

His burner phone buzzed again, a coded ping from his last remaining contact.

"Safe passage ready. South sector. Thirty minutes. Bring nothing."

Vikram's hand trembled as he pocketed the device. Gone were the polished speeches and confident grins. All that mattered now was survival.

He yanked open a battered duffel bag, checking the essentials:

A fake passport under the name "Vikram Singh";

A thick roll of unmarked cash; and

A small, bloodstained folding knife, the last line of defence.

His escape plan had been activated two hours ago: shadow operatives, bribed customs officers, and a chartered cargo flight out of the city.

But none of it felt certain anymore. Every street felt watched. Every shadow felt like a noose tightening around his throat.

***

Rajesh's urgent call cracked through Aryan's communication line.

"Vikram Sharma escaped during transport. Medical diversion compromised. Possible insider betrayal."

Aryan's face hardened instantly.

"Activate deep trace protocols," he ordered. "Full-spectrum monitoring. Every burner, every signal. Find him."

Kabir was already moving, fingers dancing over his laptop.

"Pulling emergency surveillance grids. Decrypting dark-net pings."

Aryan watched Vikram's encrypted communications stream across Kabir's decrypted dashboard.

"He's on the move," Kabir said. "Pinged a secure extraction squad in the southern sector."

Aryan's mouth hardened into a grim line. "Desperate rats always run toward the dirtiest tunnels," he said.

Naina leaned closer, eyes flashing. "Let's block every exit except the one we want him to take."

Aryan nodded once, a predator scenting blood.

Inside the mobile command van, Aryan leaned over Kabir's shoulder, watching real-time blips move across the digital grid, each dot a unit, a checkpoint, a trap. "Vikram's last ping triangulates near the old industrial quarter," Kabir said, his voice clipped and professional. "Slums to the west, abandoned factories east. He's got two routes if he wants to vanish."

Naina stood at the side, studying a secondary map.

"We bottleneck him here," she pointed at a narrow arterial lane marked in red, "and here." Her finger shifted. "Cut off southbound movement and force him toward the containment zone."

Aryan nodded, already tapping his communication unit. "Rajesh, deploy units to cross-lock the industrial exit. No sirens. I want him to feel safe, until it's too late."

"Understood," Rajesh's voice crackled back. "Units moving now."

Kabir's screen updated with new movements, white arrows flowing like streams, pinching Vikram's escape lines narrower with every passing second.

"He'll panic," Naina murmured, eyes sharp. "He always does when his control cracks."

Aryan smiled coldly. "Good. Fear makes people predictable." He checked his gear; earpiece, tactical tablet, and concealed taser.

No grand speeches now.

Just one man left to catch.

And this time, there would be no mercy.

***

The abandoned industrial yard loomed like a ghost town, rusted iron skeletons silhouetted against the misty sky.

Aryan slowed the car to a crawl, and the headlights dimmed. Beside him, Naina gripped her tablet, eyes scanning the shifting heat signatures Kabir had overlaid onto the building schematics.

"There," she whispered, pointing to a flickering red blip moving erratically near a collapsed conveyor belt.

Aryan's pulse quickened. "Vikram."

He switched off the engine. Together, they moved, low, fast, silent, shoes crunching faintly over gravel.

The yard was a labyrinth of broken machinery and sagging catwalks. Shadows shifted with every gust of the damp night breeze. Ahead, they spotted Vikram, dishevelled, frantic, weaving between rusted barrels, clutching his duffel bag like a lifeline.

Aryan raised a hand, signalling Naina to fan out.

She nodded, slipping between the skeletal beams like a phantom.

Vikram stumbled near the old loading dock. For a split second, he turned, and his eyes locked with Aryan's.

Recognition flared. Fear exploded across Vikram's face.

Aryan lunged forward. "Vikram! It's over. Don't make it worse!"

But Vikram spun around, tossing something small and metallic behind him, a flash grenade.

Instinctively, Aryan shielded his eyes as light seared the darkness, blinding and disorienting.

When the afterimages cleared, Vikram was gone; he vanished into a maze of ruined stairwells.

Aryan cursed under his breath.

Naina rejoined him, grim-faced. "He had this planned," she said. "He knows the yard better than we thought."

Aryan's fists clenched. "It doesn't matter. He's running out of places to hide."

The chase was getting uglier.

Aryan paced along the cracked asphalt outside the warehouse, mind racing faster than his heartbeat.

"We can't keep chasing him blindly," Naina said, rubbing dust from her palms. "He's unpredictable inside these ruins."

Aryan stopped short, an idea sparking.

"Exactly. That's why we stop chasing." His eyes narrowed, calculating. "We make him come to us."

Naina tilted her head, intrigued, "How?"

Kabir's voice crackled in their earpieces, full of mischief.

"You're cooking up something nasty, aren't you, bossman?"

Aryan allowed a grim smile. "Vikram still believes he has invisible hands helping him—Council friends, hidden assets. We leak just enough fake intel through those encrypted channels, a dummy safehouse he thinks he can reach."

Kabir caught on immediately. "I can bounce a false communication. Make it look like an emergency extraction code."

Naina grinned. "We bait the trap," she said, "and he'll walk right into it."

Aryan nodded. "Because panic makes people stupid."

Within minutes, Kabir was forging digital footprints, a whisper on the dark net, a scrambled message flagged 'Priority Secure'.

Coordinates: An isolated sector near an abandoned metro construction site, perfect for an ambush.

Aryan tightened his vest, checking his gear one more time. "Let's end this," he said quietly. "Vikram will think he's running to salvation, but he'll run straight into the jaws of his own destruction."

***

The old metro construction site was a graveyard of forgotten dreams, crumbling concrete pillars, rusted scaffolding, and puddles reflecting the fractured moonlight.

Aryan crouched behind a collapsed wall, his eyes locked onto the narrow dirt road leading in.

Naina was positioned opposite him, crouched low behind a skeletal metal frame, her earpiece live.

"Movement," Kabir whispered into the communication units. "One incoming. Small heat signature. It's him."

Aryan's muscles tensed.

From a distance, a lone figure emerged, hunched low, duffel bag slung across his back: Vikram.

He moved fast, half-running, half-stumbling toward the marked location.

"He took the bait," Naina murmured, sighting him through her infrared monocular.

Aryan tapped his microphone softly. "All units hold. Wait for full entry."

Through the static, Rajesh's calm voice confirmed, "Containment perimeter active. No exits."

Vikram darted under a broken beam, moving deeper into the skeleton of the construction zone, unknowingly stepping right into the kill box.

Aryan felt the slow, surgical tightening of the net.

This wasn't a chase anymore.

This was a hunt, methodical, patient, and absolute.

Vikram paused near an abandoned office trailer, glancing around nervously.

Aryan could almost hear his thoughts, the desperate hope that escape was still possible.

Naina's voice came through the unit, cool and precise. "Another thirty metres. He's fully boxed."

Aryan rose slightly, keeping to the shadows. "Wait for my signal," he said, voice like steel.

Inside the dead ruins, Vikram Sharma's empire was taking its last gasp.

Vikram stumbled into the centre of the dead zone, blinking wildly under the scattered construction lights.

He froze, realization dawning too late.

No extraction team.

No allies.

Just empty steel and silent shadows.

"Now," Aryan said into the communication unit.

From every side, silhouettes moved, commandos emerging from the ruins, rifles raised, boots crunching deliberately on the broken gravel.

Vikram spun like a cornered rat.

"No, no, no..." he muttered, backing away.

Then he spotted movement: a small boy, no older than ten, trailing after his father, one of the workers called in for temporary night duty.

In a flash of desperation, Vikram lunged.

He seized the boy, yanking him close, pressing the bloodied folding knife from his duffel against the child's throat.

The yard snapped still. The commandos froze mid-step. A collective breath held. Every finger on a trigger and every heart froze.

"Stay back!" Vikram screamed, voice shrill with terror. "You come closer, and he dies!"

Aryan cursed under his breath, raising a hand to signal a halt.

Naina slid into a tighter angle, hidden behind a fractured concrete slab, breathing steady.

Through his earpiece, Kabir whispered grimly, "He's lost it, boss. He's at the edge."

Aryan's heart pounded, but his mind remained calm.

They had expected desperation.

But this?

This was pure collapse.

Vikram's hand shook violently on the knife handle, the boy whimpering softly in terror.

One wrong move, one wrong word, and the night would end in blood.

Aryan's jaw tightened. "Time to end this, carefully."

***

Aryan moved slowly, hands raised, his voice low and steady against the charged silence.

"Vikram, listen to me," he called across the open yard. "You don't want to do this. You still have a choice."

Vikram's face twisted into something wild, broken. He jerked the boy closer, the knife trembling dangerously.

"No choices left!" he screamed. "You made sure of that!"

Aryan took another cautious step forward, his eyes locked with Vikram's.

Behind him, Naina slid into a flanking position, silent and deadly, her taser gripped loosely at her side.

"Hurting the boy won't change anything," Aryan said, his voice like iron wrapped in silk. "It'll only guarantee you never leave this yard alive."

Vikram's breath came in frantic, shallow gasps. His hand flexed involuntarily on the blade's handle.

"You don't understand!" he spat. "They'll kill me! You think you're saving anyone?"

Aryan's heart tightened.

They, the larger force behind Vikram, still hidden, still pulling strings.

"We can protect you," Aryan lied smoothly. "But not if you hurt him. You let him go, and we walk you out of here alive."

Naina was a shadow now, circling closer behind Vikram's blind side.

The boy whimpered softly.

Vikram's eyes darted around, seeing the closing circle, the inevitable end.

For a moment, just a moment, Aryan saw a brief, fatal hesitation crack the madness in Vikram's eyes.

That was the window they needed. He moved.

"Now!" Aryan barked.

In a blur of precision, Naina darted from cover, her compact taser already primed.

Vikram barely registered the movement before twin electrodes punched into his side.

Electricity arced through his body.

He convulsed violently, the knife clattering from his shaking hand. The boy screamed and stumbled away, yanked to safety by a waiting officer.

Vikram collapsed onto the gravel, twitching and gasping, the fight drained from him in an instant.

Aryan and two commandos closed in.

"Clear!" Naina shouted, rushing forward to swiftly kick away the fallen knife, sliding it away into the debris.

One of the commandos dropped to one knee beside Vikram, wrenching his arms behind his back and snapping on the flex cuffs with ruthless efficiency. Aryan stood over them, his gaze locked on Vikram's hollow stare, making sure the moment carried no illusion of escape."

Vikram groaned, dazed, blinking up at the floodlights that bathed the yard in sterile white.

"It's over," Aryan said, his voice flat. "No more running. No more hiding."

Naina stood above them, breathing hard but steady, taser still ready in her hand.

The commandos fanned out, sweeping the perimeter for any lingering threats, but it was over.

Vikram Sharma, once the architect of a hidden empire, now lay crumpled in the dust, a broken man surrounded by the very city he once thought he controlled. The fall was complete.

And justice, real justice, had finally caught up.

***

By the time Vikram was loaded into the armoured van, the first news alerts had already detonated across the city.

Kabir's voice buzzed into Aryan's earpiece, laced with grim satisfaction.

"Congratulations. You're trending, bossman. Vikram's mugshot is the face of every breaking headline."

But Aryan felt no victory, only the weight of unfinished battles.

Aryan and Naina stood side by side near the containment perimeter, reading the headlines on her tablet.

"Massive corporate scandal unfolds, TechNova executive linked to trafficking and financial fraud," one reporter shouted into her microphone, the frenzy growing by the second.

Public outrage spread like wildfire.

Social media exploded: hashtags, trending, conspiracy theories unravelling, anger boiling over in real-time.

Rajesh approached, his uniform stained with dust, but his expression grimly satisfied. "Ministry's distancing themselves already. Their official line? 'Rogue operative. Individual actions. No organizational complicity.'"

Naina snorted. "Predictable. Throw him to the wolves and burn the evidence."

Aryan nodded, eyes narrowing. "We knew they'd try to wash their hands off it."

Across the square, TechNova's damage control team fumbled through hurried press statements, trying desperately to salvage what they could from the wreckage.

But the rot was too deep.

The world had seen the truth, and no PR team could put that monster back in the cage.

The first battle was won.

The real war had just begun.

***

Inside the holding cell, under harsh fluorescent lights, Vikram Sharma sat slumped, cuffed, broken, and defeated.

Aryan leaned against the interrogation room's glass wall, arms crossed, observing silently as DCP Rajesh began the preliminary questioning.

"Who gave the orders, Vikram?" Rajesh asked, voice flat.

Vikram laughed in a hollow, cracked sound. "You think I was the mastermind?" he rasped. "You think this ends with me?"

Aryan's jaw tightened. He exchanged a knowing look with Naina, who stood beside him.

Rajesh pressed harder. "Names. Organizations. Council members. Who are they?"

Vikram leaned forward, his face a twisted mask of defiance and despair.

"You're too late," he whispered. "You think you've won? You've barely scratched the surface."

Aryan stepped into the room, calm but lethal. "No more riddles," he said quietly. "If you want to live long enough to matter, start talking."

For a moment, silence hung between them, thick, electric.

Then Vikram exhaled shakily. "There's a council," he said. "Not just businessmen. Politicians. Military contractors. Media heads. They built the pipeline I used. I was just... efficient."

Naina's pulse quickened.

Aryan's expression remained unreadable, but inside, the fire roared anew.

"What's their next move?" Aryan asked.

Vikram only smiled, bitter and broken. "You'll find out," he said softly, "when they come for you."

The air grew heavier, colder.

Aryan and Naina left Vikram to rot behind reinforced walls, but they knew this time, the battlefield would be even darker.

***

Chapter 15

REDEMPTION AND NEW BEGINNINGS

The sleek glass facade of TechNova's headquarters shimmered under the pale morning sun, but inside, the building felt hollow, its corridors stripped of their old pulse.

Aryan stepped through the main doors, the weight of expectation and uncertainty pressing down like a second skin.

Employees scattered across the lobby, whispering behind half-raised hands. Some wore hope. Others wore fear. Naina walked quietly beside Aryan, reading the tension better than any dashboard metric.

Kabir's voice buzzed into Aryan's earpiece, laced with his usual dry humour.

"Welcome back, bossman. The vultures are still circling. Media vans out front. Boardroom sharks upstairs."

Aryan exhaled slowly, scanning the marble floors that once carried his dreams.

Now, they bore the scars of betrayal and the uncertain footprints of rebuilding.

Rajesh approached from the side entrance, looking far more like a fixer than a police officer today, in civilian clothes, clean but severe.

"Internal Security sweep complete," Rajesh reported. "Communications monitored. Potential leaks isolated. You're clear to proceed."

Aryan nodded curtly. "No more second chances," he said. "Anyone involved in the cover-up, directly or indirectly, is out. Today."

Naina smiled faintly, sensing the old fire returning to Aryan's voice.

“Time to pull TechNova out of the ashes,” she said, matching his stride.

Aryan’s jaw set as they moved toward the executives’ elevator.

Outside the building, cameras flashed, news anchors rehearsed their outrage.

Inside, fear and fragile loyalty battled for dominance.

Aryan didn’t care anymore.

He had built this empire once, and he would rebuild it.

But this time, on his terms.

***

The boardroom was packed with executives, employees, and a few brave journalists allowed past security, all packed shoulder to shoulder under the harsh white lights.

Aryan stood at the podium, the company’s logo gleaming behind him like a faded relic.

For a long moment, he said nothing.

Silence gripped the room, thick, raw, expectant.

Naina stood at the side, arms folded, her gaze steady on Aryan’s face. Kabir monitored the livestream feed from a side console, fingers poised to shut it down if needed.

Aryan finally leaned into the microphone, his voice calm, deliberate.

“TechNova was built on innovation. On trust. On the idea that technology should serve people, not exploit them.”

Murmurs stirred across the room.

Aryan continued, his voice hardening.

“That trust was violated. Not by strangers, but by people inside these walls. People who sold their honour for profit.”

He let that sink in, the weight of betrayal tangible in the air.

“I take responsibility,” Aryan said, lifting his chin. “I trusted the wrong people. I overlooked warning signs. That ends today.”

Naina caught the ripple, a subtle shift in the crowd, fear giving way to cautious hope.

“We are cleaning house,” Aryan declared. “Transparent audits. Full disclosures. No more shadows. No more councils. No more silent deals. No more pretending that loyalty alone could save a dream.”

The employees shifted, some whispering, others sitting straighter.

"And if any of you are still part of the rot, leave now. Before we rip you out."

Aryan stepped back from the podium, letting the silence roar louder than any applause.

He didn't need their approval.

He needed their faith, and he had just taken the first step to earn it.

Aryan didn't waste time once the statement ended.

Within the hour, teams of internal auditors, security personnel, and Rajesh's cyber unit began moving through TechNova's sprawling corporate floors.

Naina coordinated silently from a makeshift command post two floors below the executive wing, her tablet flashing with real-time data streams.

"Start with the legal division," Aryan instructed over the encrypted channel. "Then finance. Then, supply chain management. Prioritize anyone with known ties to Vikram's sub-contracts."

Rajesh's voice crackled through, curt and efficient.

"Already cross-referencing flagged communication logs. Early signs suggest the rot goes deeper than we thought."

Aryan expected no less.

Kabir grinned from his console, his fingers dancing across the keys.

"Just dug out an off-the-books server in procurement. Hidden under a fake yoga wellness app. Extremely sneaky, these crooks."

Aryan's jaw tightened. "No second chances. Anyone even remotely involved will terminate access, retrieve evidence, and expel."

Naina's voice was calm through the communication unit.

"We're keeping this clean, Aryan. Fast, but legal. No excuses that can backfire later."

He nodded silently, appreciating her steady hand.

By mid-afternoon, seven executives had been escorted out, some quiet, some stunned, some crying, some furious.

The lower floors buzzed with rumour and relief, the loyal employees whispering behind hands, watching the cleansing with a mixture of fear and cautious pride.

This wasn't just retribution. It was a rebirth. Aryan looked over the updated security logs flashing on his tablet, names disappearing like rot being carved out of a wound.

It was messy. It was brutal.

And it was absolutely necessary.

***

The sun dipped low behind the Bangalore skyline, casting long shadows across the TechNova terrace.

Aryan leaned against the railing, staring out at the city, a city he had once believed he could change with technology alone.

Behind him, footsteps padded softly.

Naina.

She handed him a bottle of water without a word, then leaned beside him, arms folded, watching the same skyline.

For a long moment, they said nothing.

The weight of the day, of months, of betrayals, of rebuilding hung between them like a heavy mist.

Finally, Aryan broke the silence, his voice low.

"I built something meant to outlast me. Something pure."

Naina turned her head slightly, studying him. "I know," she said gently.

He let out a bitter laugh. "And I failed."

"No," Naina said quietly. "You trusted. That's different."

Aryan shook his head, a thousand regrets flickering behind his eyes.

"I should've seen it," he said. "Vikram. The cracks. The greed."

"You saw the best in people," she said. "That's not weakness, Aryan. That's why you're different."

Aryan stared down at the busy streets below.

"It almost broke me," he admitted with a sigh. "It still might."

Naina's voice was steady, cutting through the dusk. "You're still standing."

He looked at her finally, something raw and unguarded flashing across his face.

"Not alone," he said, the words heavier than he intended.

Naina offered a small smile, no bravado, no walls.

"Never alone," she echoed.

***

By the end of the week, the narrative had begun to shift.

News channels that once paraded TechNova's disgrace now aired cautious stories of its transformation.

Headlines flashed across the city's morning broadcasts:

"TechNova Cleans House: Aryan Mehra Leads Ruthless Internal Reform."

"From Scandal to Redemption? Public Opinion Wavers."

Aryan sat in the corner of the executive lounge, watching a muted news report as Naina and Kabir debriefed on the latest audit round.

The camera showed Aryan's press statement from days ago, his hard eyes, his unflinching voice now replayed with less hostility, more respect.

"They're not calling for your head anymore," Kabir grinned, tossing a folder onto the table. "Some are even calling you a 'model for corporate ethics'."

Aryan raised an eyebrow, unimpressed. "Don't believe in overnight saints," he muttered.

Naina smirked without looking up from her tablet. "But it's a start," she said.

Kabir shrugged. "Public's a funny beast," he remarked. "One minute they're lighting you on fire, the next minute they're carving your statue."

Aryan leaned back, letting the cautious relief soak in for a moment.

He wasn't naive.

This wasn't a victory.

This was survival.

The real work—regaining trust, rebuilding lives, restoring meaning—would take far longer.

But for the first time in months, there was breathing room. There was a possibility.

Aryan turned to Naina, his voice low but steady. "Let's make sure we never need a second redemption."

She smiled faintly. "Agreed," she said, eyes gleaming.

***

The next Monday morning, Aryan stood before a gathering of TechNova's remaining core team: engineers, project heads, and innovators who had survived the storm.

The conference hall was half-full, but the energy was different now, stripped of fear, raw with honesty.

No staged applause.

No hollow smiles.

Just people waiting to see if the man before them could truly lead them out of the ashes.

Aryan stepped onto the low stage, with no notes, no teleprompter, only his voice.

"I'm not going to tell you everything's fine," he began, scanning their tired, wary faces. "Because it isn't."

A ripple of uncomfortable laughter broke across the room.

He allowed a ghost of a smile before continuing.

"We were betrayed. Lied to. Used. And for that, I carry my share of blame."

The murmurs stilled.

"But what happens next is on us."

Aryan paused, letting the words anchor. Then he continued.

"No more blind obedience. No more loyalty to titles. From today, your loyalty belongs to the mission, not the men leading it. That includes me."

Naina watched from the side, arms folded, a small, approving smile tugging at her mouth.

Aryan's voice dropped lower, became intimate, almost conspiratorial.

"We rebuild from truth. From courage. From making the harder choice even when no one's watching."

Silence reigned, but it was no longer apprehensive.

It was reverent.

In that silence, something shifted, fragile but real.

Hope.

For the first time in a long time, Aryan felt it stir in the bones of the company he loved.

This wasn't resurrection through speeches.

This was healing through truth.

And it had finally begun.

***

It was late evening when Aryan returned to his temporary office, a minimalist space with bare walls and a single desk, untouched by the glamour TechNova once flaunted.

He tossed his jacket over the chair, rolling his shoulders to ease the tension.

A soft ping echoed from his encrypted terminal.

Naina, leaning against the doorway, raised an eyebrow.

"Another crisis?" she asked.

Aryan gave a humourless chuckle. "Probably."

He tapped the screen and froze.

The message wasn't internal. It was from the Global Technology Ethics Consortium, a coalition of tech visionaries, reformers, and regulators from across continents. Their message was short, formal, and heavy with implication:

"We have followed your efforts at TechNova with interest. We believe voices like yours are essential for the future of responsible technology. We invite you to join our Global Council of Ethical Innovation."

Naina crossed the room silently, to read over his shoulder.

Her reaction was a soft, amused snort.

"Well, look at that. The rebels want you on their ship."

Aryan leaned back in his chair, fingers steepled, mind already racing.

Joining meant influence.

It meant power to shape real change beyond one company.

It also meant enemies, new ones, bigger ones.

He exhaled slowly. "I didn't survive this just to fix one broken machine," he said quietly.

Naina smiled. She was not surprised. Not even slightly.

"Then maybe it's time," she said.

Aryan closed the laptop gently, a decision forming in his mind.

Time to stop surviving.

Time to start building something that couldn't be corrupted.

Not again.

Later that night, Naina sat alone in the conference room, fingers drumming lightly against her phone.

A message blinked back at her, stark, simple, impossible to ignore:

Offer from National Cyber Intelligence Directorate.

Position: Strategic Operations Lead.

Terms: Classified. Immediate Response Requested.

She leaned back, letting the phone drop onto the table.

The Directorate, a name she had only whispered about during black-ops briefings, was now knocking directly at her door.

She didn't need Aryan's insight to know what it meant: Prestige. Power. Isolation. Naina wasn't built for bureaucracy, but deep down, she knew this wasn't about status.

It was about reach.

It was about being at the frontline where real cyberwars were fought, where battles were invisible but consequences brutal.

Aryan entered quietly, reading her face with one glance.

He didn't ask. Didn't press. Just leaned casually against the door frame, arms crossed, "They want you," he said softly.

"They need me," she corrected, her voice sharper than intended.

She hadn't spent years surviving digital wars just to sit behind glass walls. She was born for storms.

A moment passed.

"And what do you want?" Aryan asked.

Naina stared at the phone for a long moment.

"I want..." she began, then stopped, because the answer wasn't simple.

A part of her craved the fight. Another part, tethered to the silent bond they had built, craved something she had never allowed herself before. Home. Trust.

Maybe even something dangerously close to peace.

She didn't answer.

Aryan didn't push.

Some decisions, they both knew, had to be made alone.

***

Aryan stood on the terrace, hands tucked into his pockets, breathing in the night air heavy with change, heavier with choices yet unspoken.

Naina joined him without a word, her presence folding into his space like a second skin.

For a long moment, they simply stood side by side, not speaking.

The silence wasn't uncomfortable. It was layered, dense with everything they had survived, everything they had built, and everything that still lingered in the spaces between them. Aryan finally broke it, his voice low, rougher than usual.

"Whatever you choose..."

Naina turned, meeting his gaze, clear, sharp, unwavering.

"...you'll have my respect," Aryan finished.

A small smile tugged at the corner of her mouth.

"And do I have yours?" She asked, the words light but the meaning heavy.

Aryan's mouth twitched, the hint of a smirk breaking through the weariness.

"You had that long before either of us noticed."

Naina's heart thudded once, hard enough to make her glance away, pretending to adjust the strap on her wristwatch.

There were no declarations between them. No grand confessions.

Just the quiet, indestructible truth:

They were each other's anchor in victory, in failure, in the dark hours when the world blurred.

And that was enough for now.

Aryan's phone buzzed, slicing through the silence.

He checked the encrypted alert, a short, urgent message from Rajesh:

"Intercepted comms. Movement detected. Council fragments regrouping. You were right, Vikram was just the beginning."

Aryan's jaw tightened. He turned the screen toward Naina. She read it in one sweep, her expression hardening immediately.

"They're not retreating," she said flatly. "They're evolving."

Aryan pocketed the phone, his mind already shifting gears from rebuilding to readiness.

"This isn't cleanup anymore," he said. "This is escalation."

Behind them, the city pulsed on, blissfully unaware of the deeper war rumbling beneath its streets, its networks, its governments.

Aryan looked at Naina, the decision unspoken but mutual.

There would be no settling.

No complacency.

Not when the council, the real architects of betrayal, were still at large, regrouping, recalibrating.

Aryan's voice cut through the heavy air, steady and unshakeable.

"Then we adapt faster."

Naina nodded once, a fierce glint in her eyes.

Across the world, the next battles were already lining up, invisible but deadly.

And this time, Aryan and Naina wouldn't just react.

They would lead.

The redemption of TechNova was only the first shot fired.

The real war was just beginning.

***

Chapter 16

A NEW FRONTLINE

The world watched and the world reacted.

In the days following Vikram Sharma's downfall and TechNova's brutal internal cleansing, headlines exploded across international news cycles:

"Corporate Redemption: TechNova Sets New Global Benchmark."

"From Scandal to Standard-Bearer: Aryan Mehra's Fight for Ethical Tech."

"Not All Are Celebrating. Shadow Networks Quietly Regroup."

Aryan sat in the modest conference room at TechNova's newly secured headquarters, scrolling through article after article.

Admiration flowed in from unexpected quarters: whistleblower groups, ethical tech startups, and international watchdogs.

But so did resentment.

Beneath the praise, Aryan could feel it:

The subtle sharpening of knives in faraway boardrooms.

The tightening of old alliances threatened by his example.

Naina entered quietly, tossing a slim folder onto the table.

"Snapshot from global intelligence reports," she said.

Aryan flipped it open.

Names. Corporations. Diplomatic cables. Some allies. Many enemies.

"They're watching us now," Naina said, voice low but steady. "And not all of them are applauding."

Aryan closed the folder carefully, meeting her gaze. "Good," he said simply.

Naina smiled a fierce, knowing smile.

Aryan had sparked a revolution inside one company.

Now, whether he wanted it or not, he had ignited something far larger.

And there was no turning back.

***

A sharp knock sounded at Aryan's office door.

Kabir poked his head in, waving a thick envelope with mock ceremony.

"Special delivery. Hand-carried by a guy in a black suit who looked allergic to smiling."

Aryan took the envelope without a word, breaking the gold-embossed seal.

Inside, a single sheet of thick, cream-coloured paper bore the insignia of the Global Tech Ethics Summit.

Naina leaned over his shoulder, reading silently.

"In recognition of your leadership in corporate reform and ethical innovation, you are formally invited to deliver the keynote address at the Global Tech Ethics Summit, Geneva."

Aryan set the letter down slowly. For a moment, the room felt smaller, the weight of expectation heavier.

"It's real," Naina said, her voice unreadable.

Kabir whistled low.

"Front page to front row. That's got to sting a few egos out there."

Aryan didn't smile. He understood exactly what the invitation meant. It wasn't just an honour.

It was a stage and a trap.

It was a platform powerful enough to amplify his ideals...or powerful enough to paint a target on his back for forces that preferred the world stay broken.

Naina watched him closely. "They wouldn't invite you if they weren't worried," she said.

Aryan met her eyes, a quiet fire sparking behind his own.

"Then it's time they have something real to worry about."

Outside, the monsoon winds battered the city, as if mirroring the gathering storm beyond TechNova's walls.

The fight had grown bigger.

And Aryan was ready to meet it head-on.

***

The rain hammered against the windows as Aryan sat alone, sifting through dossiers for the upcoming summit.

A quiet knock broke his focus.

Rajesh entered in civilian clothes, but his bearing was still all steel and precision.

Without preamble, he dropped a slim black folder onto Aryan's desk.

"Preliminary chatter from our surveillance networks," Rajesh said. His voice was low, deliberate. "You've stirred a lot more than applause."

Aryan opened the folder.

Inside were transcripts, coded communications, intercepted calls, and blurred images of discreet meetings in foreign capitals.

"They're regrouping," Rajesh continued. "The ones Vikram hinted about. The council remnants. Financial barons, political puppeteers, private militias."

Aryan scanned the data, his expression unreadable.

Rajesh leaned closer, voice sharpening.

"Some factions see your keynote speech as a threat to their very existence."

Aryan tapped a finger against the grainy photo of a familiar face, a politician once rumoured to have investments in Vikram's logistics network.

"Good," Aryan said quietly.

Rajesh didn't smile.

"This summit isn't just a podium, Aryan. It's a battlefield. And you'll be walking into it without visible armour."

Aryan closed the folder carefully, every movement measured.

"I know," he said.

Rajesh hesitated, something almost like worry flickering across his stern features.

"Be smarter than them," he said finally. "Be faster. Or you won't make it to the next fight."

Aryan had made peace with the idea of dying standing, not living kneeling. He nodded once, a silent promise between soldiers who knew the cost of standing alone.

The storm outside deepened, drumming like war drums against the glass.

Inside, Aryan's resolve hardened.

***

The rain had eased when Naina stood alone on the rooftop terrace, her phone clutched loosely in her hand.

On the screen, the Directorate's offer blinked silently, a final reminder.

High-ranking. Untouchable.

A future mapped in strategic power plays and classified corridors.

A future that didn't include Aryan.

Footsteps approached, slow and unhurried.

She didn't have to turn to know it was him.

Aryan came to stand beside her, silent, watching the slick city lights below.

"You should take it," he said quietly, after a moment.

Naina didn't reply immediately.

Instead, she let the silence stretch, feeling the weight of everything unsaid.

Finally, she spoke, her voice steady, clear.

"I'm not finished here."

Aryan turned, studying her carefully.

"This isn't your fight to carry," he said.

Naina met his gaze sharply, certain.

"It became my fight the day we chose to fix it, not walk away."

He didn't argue. He didn't smile.

He just nodded, a small, almost invisible acknowledgement of the bond that had formed between them, forged not in words, but in battle and belief.

Naina slipped her phone into her pocket, the decision made without regret.

"They'll come after you, Aryan," she said softly.

Aryan's mouth quirked in a half smile.

"They'll have to get through you first."

For the first time in weeks, Naina laughed, low and full of life.

Above them, the storm clouds broke apart, revealing a few stubborn stars clawing their way through the darkness.

***

The tarmac shimmered under the harsh Geneva floodlights, the engines of the chartered jet growling in readiness.

Aryan led the small TechNova team across the asphalt, their footsteps steady despite the undercurrent of gathering storms.

Naina moved alongside him, her gaze sharp, reading the quiet hostility in the glances from nearby officials and security staff.

They carried no weapons.

Only evidence.

Only truth.

And sometimes, that was the most dangerous cargo of all.

As they reached the boarding stairs, Kabir jogged up with a grin, slinging a hardened case onto his shoulder. "Hope you packed light," he joked. "We might not be coming back through customs."

Aryan allowed a flicker of a smile, brief and knowing.

At the foot of the steps, a legal aide hurried up to them, slipping an unmarked envelope into Aryan's hand.

Inside was a simple typed message:

"Withdraw quietly. Or you won't have another chance."

Aryan crumpled the note without breaking stride.

Fear was a tool. They had used it against others for years. Now it was their turn to be afraid.

He glanced sideways at Naina.

"Still sure?" he asked softly.

Naina smirked, the fierce light in her eyes undimmed.

"Always."

They climbed the steps without looking back.

The engines roared to life, a deep, relentless sound that swallowed the night.

As the jet lifted into the dark, uncertain skies, Aryan felt no hesitation.

They weren't running.

They were advancing.

Toward Geneva.

Toward the council.

Toward the next war.

And this time, they would be ready.

***

Glossary

This glossary explains some technical and security terms referenced throughout the story to aid the readers' understanding.

DDoS Attack: A Distributed Denial of Service attack, where hackers flood a server with excessive traffic to crash or disable it.

Encryption: The process of converting data into a secure code to prevent unauthorized access or tampering.

Checksum: A sequence of numbers or data used to verify the integrity of information, ensuring it has not been altered.

Dark Net: A hidden part of the internet that operates anonymously and is often associated with illegal activities.

Blockchain Verification: A secure method of confirming transactions or data records using a decentralized and tamper-proof digital ledger.

Data Vault: A highly secure and encrypted storage system used to safeguard critical digital evidence.

Biometric Identifier: A physical trait, such as a fingerprint, retina scan, or facial recognition, used for verifying a person's identity.

Dummy Corporation: A fake or shell company created to hide illegal activities, money laundering, or secret transactions.

Trafficking Networks: Underground criminal systems that illegally move people, goods, or sensitive materials across regions.

Forensic Audit: An in-depth investigation into financial records, aimed at detecting fraud, embezzlement, or other criminal activities.

Payload: In cybersecurity, the part of malware or a hacking programme that executes the intended harmful action.

Satellite Feed: Real-time data or imagery transmitted from satellites, often used for surveillance or intelligence purposes.

Council: A secret coalition of powerful figures, politicians, corporate magnates, and military contractors orchestrating hidden agendas and global manipulation.

Coded Chatter: Encrypted or disguised communications, often intercepted by intelligence agencies to detect covert operations.

Taser: A non-lethal weapon that incapacitates a person temporarily by delivering an electric shock.

Whistleblower: A person who exposes hidden, unethical, or illegal activities within an organization to the public or authorities.

Command Protocols: Pre-defined sets of instructions or operational plans activated during emergencies, especially in security and law enforcement settings.

Extraction Team: A specialized unit tasked with rescuing or evacuating individuals from dangerous situations.

Neutralization: In security or intelligence contexts, this means eliminating or rendering a threat harmless legally, digitally, or tactically.

Acknowledgements

This story was forged in the rhythms of policing—operations rooms, the digital grind of intelligence against jungle and urban naxals, rain-slick highways, and long night hours of strategy with seniors and colleagues. While The Bangalore Conspiracy is fiction, the grit, hope, and human dilemmas within it come from years of service and the privilege of participating and witnessing courage at close quarters.

My first and deepest sashtang pranam to Sh Guru Maharaj Ji "Srimad J.G.R. Swami Shri Purushottamacharya Ji Maharaj" whose serene smile, blessings, and unseen grace kept the path lit.

To my Maa and Papa, I am here because of you, whatever I have become rests on your sacrifices.

This book was written during demanding office hours at CRPF Headquarters, New Delhi—a portfolio that left little spare time and even less energy to think. In that narrow space, my family became the oxygen. Babita my wife; Aarjav, my son; and Arushi, my daughter—your patience, love, and gentle insistence that I kept writing formed the spine of this work. Aarjav, your sharp notes and long discussions on AI and the digital world shaped by your studies at ISB Hyderabad and experience as an AI Product Manager kept the tech heart of this thriller honest and contemporary.

Behind the scenes, heartfelt thanks to my brother Amit and my sister Kamana, to colleagues who offered clear-eyed critiques, and to friends whose curious nudges and early-draft feedback propelled me forward.

To my CRPF fraternity, officers, ranks, veterans, and families—thank you for the insights, stories, and quiet strength that only service can teach. Whatever rings true here belongs to you, all views and any errors are mine alone.

My gratitude to Arup Bose of Srishti Publishers and his dedicated team for believing in this manuscript and steering it from draft to book. Warm thanks to Suhail Mathur and the team at The Book Bakers for mentoring me through the modern craft and business of writing and publishing, from pitch to press.

To every colleague who stood with me in difficult hours, and every family that waited through them—this book remembers you.

Jai Hind.